BENSON'S BUTTE

Benson's Butte had been a prosperous cow town until over-grazing and disease ruined the cattle business. When Bill Quince rides into town looking for work, a visiting government surveyor employs him to help re-map the area. An ambitious banker and most of the ranchers conspire to exploit the situation to their own advantage. Just one rancher holds out. He hates Benson's Butte and has his own plans for the town. Bribery, treachery — and murder — are the order of the day.

Books by Will Parr
in the Linford Western Library:

THE LONG REVENGE

WILL PARR

BENSON'S BUTTE

Complete and Unabridged

LINFORD
Leicester

First published in Great Britain in 1998 by
Robert Hale Limited
London

First Linford Edition
published 2001
by arrangement with
Robert Hale Limited
London

British Library CIP Data

Parr, Will
    Benson's Butte.—Large print ed.—
Linford western library
1. Western stories
2. Large type books
I. Title
823.9'14 [F]

ISBN 0–7089–4547–3

Published by
F. A. Thorpe (Publishing)
Anstey, Leicestershire

Set by Words & Graphics Ltd.
Anstey, Leicestershire
Printed and bound in Great Britain by
T. J. International Ltd., Padstow, Cornwall

1

The man who rode slowly into town was gaunt and badly in need of a shave. He sat tall on the raw-boned horse that trudged wearily on loose shoes which clattered each time a hoof was put down on the dusty main street. The man on its back was covered in a pale layer of trail dirt and his worn shirt and pants were patched and sweat-stained. His waistcoat was leather, cracked and scuffed, with no buttons, and the string of a tobacco pouch stuck out of one pocket. He held the rein loosely, his thin young face drawn under the old stetson that was frayed round the edges and bleached white by the sun.

He carried no guns, but a rolled blanket was tied behind the saddle. A water bottle bounced against the horse's flank and worn saddle-bags lay on either side of the crupper. Nobody in Benson's Butte paid much attention to the stranger. It was a small town, without curiosity, and with a shrinking population since the price of beef had fallen and local pasturage had deteriorated over the last few storm-ridden seasons.

The saloon, which doubled as a hotel, lay on the visitor's left. It was a two-storey frame building with an assortment of old chairs on the porch. A few of them were occupied by regulars who watched events in the town, barely moving their lips in dull conversation. A bank lay further along on the same side, next to a bath house, and almost opposite a dry goods store that needed its windows cleaning so that the items on display could be seen to better advantage.

The stranger lifted a gloved hand to block out the low afternoon sun and peered ahead to make out the blacksmith's sign at the far end of the main street. It lay on the right, a little away from the other buildings and was also a livery stable with two corrals alongside it that abutted on to a feed store. The tired horse seemed to sense that the journey was at an end and its head rose a little as it responded to the clicking noise made by the rider to hustle it along.

Double gates fronted the smithy, permanently open and hanging from rusty iron hinges that were no credit to a worker in metal. A forge glowed brightly in the gloom beyond the doors, and the smith was sitting on the anvil, drinking coffee. He was a tall man, running to fat and potbellied. His face was melancholy and fringed by greying whiskers. His eyes were a startling blue as he watched the stranger dismount and lead the horse to the gates of the smithy.

'Howdy,' he greeted his solitary customer, 'and what can I be doin' for you?'

'Shoes need lookin' at,' the stranger replied in a quiet, rather hesitant voice.

'I can soon fit you a new set. No trouble.'

'Well . . . I'm not so sure I can afford that. The front right is in bad need of renewin', but I'd be much obliged if you could just tighten up the others.'

The smith put down his mug on the anvil and came out into the daylight. He checked each foot of the horse silently and then nodded agreement.

'Can do,' he conceded. 'Won't last for long, but should put you over for a week or so. You look as if you've travelled some ways.'

The stranger grinned silently, displaying surprisingly good teeth. 'From just south of Medicine Bow,' he admitted with a vague touch of pride. 'I sure figure that to bein' some ways, at least, by my reckoning.'

The smith whistled between his bad teeth. 'I'm sure it is, fella. Close on eighty miles, I'd guess. But if it's work you'd be lookin' for, I have to tell you that this town is not the place.'

The other man shrugged. 'I'm a cattle hand, I don't want town work. I was kinda hopin' that some of the ranchers in the area might still need a little experienced help.'

The smith shook his head gently. 'No hopes, man,' he said. 'With all this bad grazin' after the hard winters we've had lately, and these fancy-named cattle diseases, there ain' no tradin' worth a damn. We're all survivin' on what's left of things. I'd move on if I was a mite younger, but I got me a wife and kids and nobody will buy this business at any price. From what I hear tell, it's like this throughout the territory.'

'Yeah, I reckon so. I'm figurin' to head south for Colorado after I've rested up a few days.'

'They got themselves a lotta sheep down there, so they tell me,' the smith ventured with a sly look.

'If sheep's all that's on offer, I might even consider them,' the stranger said meekly.

'Well, don't let the folk round here know you're that desperate. Sheep ain't a welcome thing to talk about. The ranchers are blamin' the sheep men and the Homestead Act for all their troubles. I reckon as how they're wrong, but it ain't for me to be takin' sides. All the same, my very best customers have always been the cattle men. They was real big spenders in town when times were good.'

The stranger nodded his thanks. 'I'll keep my mouth closed around town,' he promised, 'but I'll need to find me some sort of lodging. Can you look after my horse?'

'Sure can, and I'll feed him good for you. Ma Riley's saloon is the only respectable place in Benson's Butte and she keeps a good table. That's always supposin' as how you have the ready cash money.'

'I doubt if I can afford hotel prices . . . '

The smith jumped in quickly. 'I can put you up in the barn. Plenty of clean straw and a good privy out beyond the stable. Real cheap, too. My wife's a fine plain cook. Nothin' fancy but plenty wholesome.'

'I reckon that'll do me right fine.'

The smith took the reins of the horse and led it into the dimness of the forge.

'And what name would you be havin'?' he asked.

'Quince,' the man answered as he untied his blanket roll and saddle-bags. 'Bill Quince. Originally from Idaho.'

'I'm Macy. Just plain Macy. Even my wife and kids call me nothing else. Came here twenty years ago after the war finished and when things were lookin' real good. The cattle were always on the move to the big towns and we had ourselves a nice little life. Plenty of work, good neighbours and a feelin' of security. The ranchers and their hands spent money aplenty and I looked after one hell of a lot of horses. Bought out the livery stable when old Charlie retired, and did a good line in fencin' too. Brazin' and shapin' all the iron work.'

'I thought it was free range in Wyomin'?'

The blacksmith grinned and spat

accurately into the fire.

'Most of it is, but there are some fenced-in places owned by the older families. Up along the creek and over beyond the butte. They were the early ones. Came here fifty years or more when there were still Indians and no railroad across the territory. No law, either. So even folks without any rights got to fencin' in land. This new legislature has spoiled things for a lotta folk. Only real land owners like the Bensons and the Winfields still fence in some ranges for their private use.'

'And what about the railroad? How far would that be from Benson's Butte?'

Macy shrugged his shoulders. 'Too far to do us any good,' he said ruefully. 'Thirty to forty miles, I guess. And the trains don't stop until they reach Chugwater. Things might have been a mite different if we'd had a rail through town. But I reckon they thought that Benson's Butte wasn't big enough, or perhaps the politicians in Cheyenne had their own plans.'

He patted the horse on its flank and the animal shuddered with pleasure.

'One day, perhaps,' he murmured, 'but I reckon we won't get rails in my lifetime.'

He led his lodger over to the barn and pointed out the amenities.

Bill Quince had a meal with the Macy family, sharing a bare room that smelled of greasy bacon and oil from a lamp that hung from the rafters. He laid out his blankets among the sweet-smelling straw in the barn and had a shave in cold water, the blunt razor rasping angrily across his cheeks. It made him feel better, though and he took off to find himself a nice long glass of beer to finish off the first day in a new town.

Dusk had come quickly and a pale moon was rising over the distant butte after which the little cluster of buildings was named. The temperature had dropped rapidly with the setting of the sun and there was a chill wind that blew little swirls of grit and sand across the main street. A few people were about and the lights shone behind the windows of the wooden buildings. The moon was throwing deepening shadows and Ma Riley's saloon flung out a cheerful welcome of pink and yellow-shaded oil lamps that decorated the two large windows on either side of the wide swing doors.

Bill Quince licked his lips and felt for the small change in his waistcoat pocket. He could afford a beer or two before settling down for the night. He shivered slightly in the cold wind and hurried up the creaking wooden steps into the warmth of the saloon.

The interior of the place was a little better than he expected. There were clean tables and chairs with a few decently dressed townsmen sitting at their drinks or playing cards quietly. The long bar was over against the far left wall, with a large gilded mirror behind it and several shelves of nearly empty spirit bottles that looked as if they were seldom moved. Most of the drinkers were sitting or standing with glasses of cheap beer in front of them and the place was empty enough for the solitary bartender to be standing idly watching four elderly men playing poker for very small stakes at a nearby table.

Bill Quince crossed to the bar under the stares of people no longer used to seeing strangers in the saloon. The bartender moved back behind the counter and silently served the beer for which he was asked. He took note of how carefully the newcomer dealt out the coins and he transferred them to the drawer with a slight expression of contempt on his long, lugubrious face. His job done, he wiped over the bar top with a damp cloth and went back to watch the poker game.

The newcomer sipped the beer slowly, trying to make it last so that he could enjoy the warmth and light of the saloon for as long as possible before going to the smithy barn and the bed of straw. He paid little attention to the noise of wagon wheels outside and had his back turned when the doors of the saloon swung open to admit two men who strode purposefully to the bar and ordered beer. They were obviously ranch hands with lean, tanned faces and plaid wool shirts that were worn but clean. Their boots were dusty from the trail and each carried a serviceable-looking Colt at his hip.

The younger of the two men was freshly shaven and had pale hair that was slicked down with pomade. He looked ready for a night of enjoyment away from the chores of the day. He took a large swig from his glass and stared casually around the bar, nodding his head to one or two people he seemed to know. They returned the greeting without enthusiasm. Then his pale eyes lit upon Bill Quince.

There was puzzlement on his face for a moment and then the cold eyes narrowed and he put down the glass with a bang. Everyone looked up from what they were doing and his companion opened his mouth in surprise.

'What's up, Pete?' he asked anxiously.

The younger man removed the clip that covered the top of the holstered gun. His crudely handsome face was set in a belligerent glare.

'I just seen me a skunk who needs a little hangin',' he said bleakly.

He was looking steadily at Bill Quince and nobody in the bar could doubt the identity of the man he was describing.

Bill Quince put down his own drink and moved slightly away from the counter.

'If that's meant for me,' he said calmly, 'you're on dangerous territory, mister. We've never met, as I recall.'

Pete Saker nodded agreement. 'If we had, you'd be dead,' he blustered, 'but you was pointed out to me along Chugwater Creek, and I've a good memory for faces.'

His hand went down to the butt of the Colt and everyone in the saloon automatically ducked for cover.

'He's not carryin' a gun!' someone yelled, amid all the upsetting of chairs.

Pete's pistol was already in his hand, his thumb drawing back the hammer. The strident voice made him hesitate for a moment and, in that split second, Bill Quince's fist caught the ranch hand in the throat with brutal force.

The Colt dropped to the floor and Quince scooped it up before anyone else got ideas about drawing. Pete Saker's companion, short and stockily built, moved his own hand well away from his holster and tried the effect of an ingratiating smile.

'I'm not in this,' he explained with a fine display of large, tombstone teeth that were well spaced out in his wide mouth. 'This is Pete's fight.'

'Then take him to a doctor,' Quince advised calmly. 'I hit him hard and he's not goin' to be too conversational for quite a time.'

★ ★ ★

Pete Saker was kneeling on the sawdusted floor by now, rocking backwards and forwards and emitting loud groans as he massaged his neck with large, rough hands. His nervous companion helped him to his feet and they made their way out of the saloon watched silently by the other drinkers who seemed to have little sympathy to offer. Bill Quince waited until he heard the wagon wheels recede, and then placed the Colt on the bar top.

'You can give it back to him when he recovers,' he told the bartender.

The man nodded silently and placed the firearm under the counter. He also picked up a clean spirit glass and filled it with whiskey.

'On the house,' he said shortly.

Bill Quince nodded his thanks.

A few minutes passed by and the conversation in the saloon gradually returned to normal. The bartender had gone to the bottom of a flight of carpeted stairs at the opposite end of the room and exchanged a few words with a stout woman who came down to meet him. She was plain, with grey hair neatly tied in a bun at the nape of her white neck. Her dress was pale lilac with white lace facings and she surveyed the room with a calm, almost judicial expression. Her head turned as she listened to the bartender and a very slight smile twitched the corners of her tiny, pinched mouth. For one moment, she looked over in the direction of Quince and favoured him with a small gesture of the right hand. Then she went back up the stairs, a regal figure secure in her own authority.

Another man entered the bar while this ritualistic exchange took place. He was short with a prominent belly and a round, red face that sprouted a grey, unkempt moustache. His nose was peeled with the sun and short-sighted blue eyes peered out from under a wide-brimmed hat that sported a silver sweatband. He carried a shotgun in the crook of his arm. It was a dangerous-looking weapon with a sawn-off barrel and his stubby fingers were close to the trigger guard.

A wide belt held a Colt .44 with a yellowing ivory butt that was engraved with initials. The man glanced slowly round the room, and then his rheumy eyes rested on Bill Quince. He went slowly across to him and laid the shotgun noisily on the counter.

'I'm told you had a run-in with Pete Saker,' he said, in a deep, gravelly voice. 'The doc is busy patchin' him up right now. Got a real job on there, I reckon.'

Quince put down his drink and looked at the man silently for a moment.

'Would you be the law around here?' he asked quietly.

The newcomer looked startled for a moment and then glanced down at his open leather waistcoat.

'Town marshal,' he confessed modestly. 'And I reckon I forgot to put on my badge again. Don't usually seem necessary seein' as all these folks know me pretty well. The name is Sawyer, Matt Sawyer. You can call me Marshal

Sawyer. Till you gets to know me better, that is.'

'Well, Marshal, how can I be of help to you?'

The lawman glanced slowly round the saloon and addressed Bill Quince in a quieter, more conspiratorial tone.

'I figure that you did a very good job on Pete,' he said, 'him bein' armed an' all.' There was admiration in his voice.

Bill Quince took a sip of beer. 'You've seen him?' he asked.

'Sure have, down at Doc Merton's house. You busted up his speakin' parts pretty good, so the old quack tells me. He'll be on slops for a coupla months or more. His sidekick says that Pete drew on you. Happen to know why?'

The other man shrugged. 'Said he knew me from some place. When I told him to back off, he got real edgy, so I had to disarm him.'

'And a mighty fine job you did, stranger,' the marshal agreed. 'Had he seen you before?'

'Not that I can recall, but he seemed

to have a real hate for me. Can't think why.'

'I was havin' a word with Macy.'

'Macy?'

'Your landlord and our blacksmith.'

'Oh, yeah.'

'And he tells me that you're just driftin' through lookin' for work with cattle. Got no money, no guns, and a broken-down old cowpony. True?'

'More or less. I had to sell my carbine and a good Colt in order to eat. I'm just restin' up and havin' my horse cared for, then I'll get out of your hair. I'm not lookin' to be troublin' nobody.'

The marshal nodded his satisfaction. 'Movin' on might be a good notion. Pete Saker will be lookin' for you once he gets over his troubles. And he won't worry about you not carryin' a gun. He'd as soon shoot a man in the back. Pete's the kinda low-life who reckons that's the best way to get even.'

Qince managed a tight smile. 'He doesn't sound popular,' he said.

'He ain't. Not with nobody. But that

don't make him any the less dangerous. He came into town tonight to collect some supplies from the dry goods store, and he was reckonin' on a few drinks, a friendly whore, and a bit of trouble-makin' before he went back to the ranch. He made the mistake of putting those chores in the wrong order. He won't forget you, stranger, so you'd best watch yourself.'

Quince nodded. 'His friends at the ranch?' he asked. 'Will they come lookin' for me too?'

'Not unless they've a mind to buy you a drink,' the marshal grinned. 'The Pete Sakers of the world don't have friends. He's only got work because he's good with cattle and handy in a fight with sheep farmers if they're fool enough to come into the area.'

Bill Quince hesitated for a moment and then decided to take the plunge.

'Would you care to take a glass of somethin' with me, Marshal?' he asked.

The older man grinned. 'I was thinkin' you was never goin' to ask,' he said happily. 'I'll take a glass of beer. It's a bad day when the town marshal has to buy his own drinks. A poor day for civilized livin'. But can you afford it, son?'

'Oh, I can manage another few beers.'

'Good, then I'll be happy to join you. Many a troublemaker has kept himself from spendin' a night in my jailhouse by makin' a gesture like that. Saves trouble all round when it's just a bit of boisterous fun.'

The bartender silently served the two men and returned to watching the poker game. The marshal took an appreciative sip from the glass and wiped his ragged moustache with the back of a gnarled hand.

'Where is it you come from, son?' he asked casually.

'I was . . . '

Quince never got a chance to finish the sentence. The double doors of the saloon flew open with startling noise and Pete Saker stood on the threshold with a gun in each hand.

2

Saker's face was pale and drawn. His eyes appeared to be out of focus and there was saliva at the corners of his mouth. His throat was wrapped round with a wide, white bandage that gave him the look of a demented preacher-man. He held the two Colts unsteadily as he swayed on his feet across the saloon. The marshal swore under his breath and made to draw his own pistol. Pete gave vent to a violent growling from his damaged throat and gestured with one of the guns. The marshal wisely decided not to do anything silly and spread out his hands in a friendly manner.

'Come on now, Pete,' he said in the crooning voice of a father talking round a naughty child. 'Stop actin' like a sick gopher and put them pieces away. I don't want to jail you while you've gotten yourself a perfectly good bed at the doc's house. Just put 'em down, lad.'

He was eyeing the shotgun that lay on the bar near his left elbow. Bill Quince stood rigidly at the marshal's side as though his very passivity would save him from the hysterical rage of the intruder.

Pete Saker advanced towards the centre of the room, his footsteps hesitant and as heavy as lead. He levelled the gun in his right hand and pointed it waveringly at Quince. Grunts tumbled from his damaged throat all the time, bringing more froth to the edges of his mouth. He pulled back the hammer with some difficulty and the noise it made echoed round the silent bar.

'Pete, for God's sake!' the marshal tried again. 'I'll have to kill you, boy, if you pull that trigger!'

Pete stared at the lawman with a face that betrayed no sense or understanding. His eyes were blank and he appeared totally unable to focus them. He swayed to within six feet of the man at the bar and stood with his legs apart and his right arm braced to shoot. The Colt jerked angrily in his hand as he sank slowly to his knees and knelt as though in prayer while the marshal gently removed both pistols from his grasp and breathed a noisy sigh of relief. He put the Colt back on half-cock and placed both guns on the bar next to his shotgun.

'I reckon you and me nearly got ourselves killed back there, son,' he said quietly. 'I'll take him along to the jailhouse now and he can sleep it off.'

He began hoisting the man to his feet as the town doctor fussily entered, his frockcoat tails flying and a pair of carpet slippers on his feet.

'He got plumb away from us,' he panted, 'clean out of the house while we were having a cup of coffee. Anyway, there's no harm done. The morphia seems to have taken effect.'

He mopped his brow cheerfully with

a large and none-too-clean handker-
chief and helped the marshal place Pete
Saker in a chair. The cowboy now
looked as if he was fast asleep as his
body sagged across the table. The
doctor stood proudly admiring his
handiwork.

He was a very short, stout man, with
a round, healthy face and bald head
that was fringed with a halo of fine
white hair. Gold spectacles hung from a
cord that was attached to the lapel of
his coat and his shirt front was streaked
with cigar ash.

'Doc, you sure as hell are one responsible
citizen,' the marshal growled angrily.
'I'd have been a damned sight happier
if your morphy stuff had acted a lot
earlier. He nearly goddamn killed us!
And where in hell's name did he get
two guns?'

'My fault, I'm afraid,' the doctor
admitted happily. 'They were on the
shelf in my office. One of my clients
paid his bill with them. Got the holsters
too.'

The marshal looked round the room as if appealing for moral support. All he got were wide grins.

'Somebody brings you a cowpoke who's just been tryin' to kill a fella and you leave him in your goddamn surgery with a couple of Colts! Doc, I should lock you up as a public nuisance. Haven't you got the sense you was born with?'

The doctor felt in his waistcoat pocket for a small stogey and looked round for someone to give him a light. When nobody offered, he lit it himself with a vesta from a small silver box.

'They weren't loaded, you jackass,' he said complacently. 'I'm a respected and responsible member of the medical profession, not the third-rate marshal of some hick town at the back-end of nowhere. Do you imagine that I'd leave loaded guns around when I treat so many gunshot wounds? If you wore eyeglasses, like every man of your age should, you'd have seen there were no bullets in them.'

The marshal flushed angrily for a moment and then grinned at what was obviously the sally of an old opponent.

'All right, so you win this round, you old quack,' he said cheerfully, 'but if that morphy stuff hadn't worked when it did, you might have been treatin' a few more gunshot wounds. Mine among them. I nearly had to draw on that varmint. He could have been killed.'

Nobody had the nerve to point out that the marshal had been at a certain disadvantage when Pete was waving a gun around.

'More likely he'd have killed you. Don't worry, Matt, he was nearly out on his feet. I'm surprised he even got as far as the saloon. I'd stuck him with nearly half a grain of the stuff. That would put out a buffalo, given enough time.'

'Stuck him!' The marshal shuddered. 'You mean that you put one of them needle things in him? I reckon that's as bad as bein' scalped. Even I don't hate the sidewindin' skunk that much.'

'It's modern medicine, you old nannygoat. If I'd fed that fellow half a grain of morphine by mouth, he'd sure as hell still be raging around. Now, let's get him back to my place where he can sleep it off, then he can go back to the ranch in the morning for a long rest-up. He's got a few nasty weeks ahead of him with a voice box that's all disconnected like. I've never had a case like this before and I don't know a medical term for it.'

He glared at Bill Quince.

'Are you the fellow who slugged him?'

'Yep.'

'Hell, you've got one hell of a punch, mister.'

'It saved his life,' the marshal said dryly.

'I'm not saying it didn't, but he's spoiled Pete Saker's chances of getting into the church choir.'

He turned to the assembled company who had listened to the exchanges with considerable interest and amusement.

'If some of you able-bodied panty-waists could grab an arm and a leg here and there, we might get this sleeping beauty to my office,' he shouted cheerfully. 'In return for which service, my lady wife may regale each one of you with a small glass of sarsaparilla.'

There was an immediate rush of volunteers because the doctor was popular and his particular brand of sarsaparilla tasted uncannily like whiskey. The unconscious Pete Saker was unceremoniously hoisted between six slightly intoxicated regulars and borne from the saloon, followed by the doctor who waved an airy good night to those who remained behind. The marshal returned to his drink and Bill Quince joined him.

'Interestin' sort of town you have here, Marshal Sawyer,' the stranger said with a slight smile.

'Well, you're helpin' to make it so, lad,' the lawman agreed, 'but the old fightin' days are long gone. Not so many ranch hands comin' in after a cattle drive or a round-up. There just ain't the steer money here any more.'

'Yes, Mr Macy told me. The whole territory seems to have had a few bad years. Those storms last season, they were the worst I ever remember. Real bad.'

'Bad! They were the work of the Devil, son. And Benson's Butte has suffered more than most. If we'd had the railroad goin' through, it mighta helped, but you can't drive cattle all the way to Chugwater and Cheyenne unless there's enough pasture on the way. We've had three real cruel winters now, and the grass just ain't there any more. So the ranchers are cuttin' down their herds, layin' off hands, and spendin' less money. That affects the whole town, so everybody suffers. Of course, nobody will admit to overgrazin' or not killin' off cattle quickly enough when they get diseased, but somethin' sure has ruined things for all of us. I used to have two deputies in the old days. Needed 'em, too. Now, I can run things all by myself.'

He looked slyly at his companion.

'The town would still run to one deputy if anyone was interested,' he said slowly.

'Meanin' me?'

'Maybe. I reckon you can handle yourself. It's poor money, but you get board and lodgin'. I can fix you up with a shotgun, a Winchester carbine, and a .44 Colt. Of course, I'd have to make a check on your background. Just routine, you understand. Lawmen can't be perfect or they wouldn't be gunslingers in the first case.'

'Thanks, I'll think about it, Marshal,' Bill Quince answered. 'I might be right glad of the offer.'

'You give it some thought, son. I'll have to retire one day soon and a good deputy who had my backing would almost certainly walk straight into the job. I reckon I've got some influence with the town council.'

Bill Quince looked round the room.

'It's a Saturday night,' he said quietly, 'and most towns would have a pretty busy saloon right now, a lotta drunks and a few fights. I reckon a deputy marshal's life in Benson's Butte could be a mighty quiet one.'

The marshal nodded his agreement.

'A dull life maybe, but a long one,' he said. 'Only one stage each month: no telegraph nearer than Cheyenne or Little Bear; no Indians runnin' wild, and no drunken cowpokes lookin' for trouble. Not a bad town for a lawman.'

'Except for Pete Saker.'

'Son, if you was wearin' a marshal's badge, Pete Saker would be singin' mighty small. 'Sides, he ain't in town all that often. So, think it over. You could do one hell of a lot worse than end your days in Benson's Butte.'

He raised a quizzical eyebrow. 'If you do accept and I have to start checkin' on your past, I hope there's nothin' that you wouldn't like a lawman to hear?'

Bill Quince smiled. 'No, Marshal,' he said. 'My family are just ordinary folks, I reckon.'

'Then tell me 'bout yourself, son.'

'Well, I was born in Idaho. My ma and pa were movin' gradually West to make somethin' of their lives, and the old man always had ambition to run cattle up somewhere near the Snake River area. He had some relatives who'd done well for themselves that way. But Ma and Pa never raised enough money, or perhaps they ran outa spirit. Leastways they ended up in Eagle Rock and Pa took on the job of toll collector up at the end of the Idaho Falls canyon. They never moved no further, so when they died of lung congestion there was nothin' for me but makin' out on my own. I could ride and shoot and handle cattle. So that was what I did.'

'Did you get any schoolin'?'

'Never did go to school very much. We was too far away from one. I can't read or write and I can't figure too well. Does a lawman have to have book learnin'?'

'Not really. We even have judges out here who can't read a law book or add

33

up the fines they hand out. I reckon a deputy marshal can manage if more important folk is just as ignorant. Of course, it helps to read and write, and there's a lot to be said for it, I'll admit to that. Just look at Doc Merton now. He reads books. That's how he learned to stick needles in folks and dress in a frock coat and a beaver hat. So, what happened next?'

'I worked for Mr Frane on the WF spread, down by the Lower Snake River until he died and the ranch was divided up between his sons. Most of us got paid off then. The spreads were too small to need as many hands. I've moved around since that time, taking whatever was on offer.'

'And your last job?'

'As Pete Saker said, I was at Chugwater Creek on the Emerson spread. It was good there but old man Emerson had to cut down his herd when the grazin' went bad. He also lost a lotta steers through disease.'

The marshal nodded. 'Yeah, it's the

same story all over. But at least the folks around Chugwater have the railroad to help them. All right, son, if you decide to accept my offer, let me know and I'll make me a check on your background. If you come out with a reasonably clean sheet, you got yourself a job here.'

3

The monthly stagecoach arrived a couple of days later. It careered into the town amid a halo of reddish dust and with the guard throwing gravel at the steaming backs of the horses to give the locals the impression of speed and urgency. He also bellowed at the animals as if in encouragement. Benson's Butte was only a short stop and, although the horses were getting tired, they still had a few miles to go before being exchanged at a ranch up near the creek. The lumbering vehicle rolled to a halt outside the bank, which also served as ticket sales office and Wells Fargo depot. The elderly clerk came running out as a few people gathered to view one of the few novelties that disturbed the dullness of everyday life in the town.

Only one passenger alighted and

waited patiently for his luggage to be passed down to the wooden sidewalk. Two people got on, a depressed-looking couple with an assortment of bags that took the efforts of the driver and the guard to get stowed away. Some mail for the town was handed to the bank clerk and he and the driver exchanged a few words of gossip before the horses were whipped up again. The guard yelled his shrill encouragement as the stage rattled away to leave Benson's Butte cut off from the rest of the world for another month. It was all over in a few minutes and only a haze of dust was left to show that there had ever been a disturbance in the routine of the town.

The newcomer was neatly dressed in a dark broadcloth coat and doeskin waistcoat. He wore a low-crowned hat and took it off to wipe the dust from his cheeks. He was a man in his fifties, broad and solid-looking, with a pale face and slightly sagging jawline. His hair was plentiful, streaked grey and curling low on his forehead. He sported a slight moustache that was neatly trimmed as were his symmetrical sideburns. The locals would have thought him something of a dude and, like many a dude, he did not appear to be carrying a gun. There were two large leather bags at his feet, both very tightly packed and one of them containing some sort of wooden contraption that stuck out at either end of the bag.

His elegant presence provoked a vague curiosity and he raised his hat politely to a couple of elderly ladies who came across from the opposite sidewalk to deliberately pass him by and get a closer look at this rather handsome, middle-aged stranger who dressed so well.

He looked around with perfect composure before picking up his luggage and heading for Ma Riley's saloon. It was practically empty so early in the day and the bartender whispered a few words in the ear of Ma Riley herself who was standing at the cash drawer, counting out some small change. She came hurriedly round the counter to greet the stranger, her dumpy face wreathed in an artificial smile of welcome. He took off his hat politely and enquired for a room.

'And how long would you be wantin' it for?' she asked, as if rooms in Benson's Butte were a commodity of considerable value and not easily to be had.

'Oh, I should say that I would need it for a week or two, ma'am,' the stranger answered in a rich baritone. 'I have a little mission to fulfil in your lovely town and I would estimate that two weeks would suffice.'

Ma blinked. Nobody had ever described Benson's Butte as lovely, and she was intrigued by the well-bred, gentlemanly qualities of her new tenant. Her shrewd eyes had already taken in the gold watch chain and the cut of the expensive clothes.

'I think we can fit you in nicely, sir,' she said in her most genteel manner.

'I'll have the bags taken up to your room. You'll want to get settled in after that awful stage.'

Her voice rose to a penetrating shriek.

'Fred! Take the gentleman's bags up to number four,' she bawled.

She then turned back smilingly to the stranger, her tones as mellow as previously.

'And what name would I be puttin' in the book then?' she asked.

'My card, dear lady.'

The gentleman took a piece of pasteboard from his waistcoat pocket with something of the flourish of a stage conjuror and passed it over to her. Ma Riley looked at the copperplate engraving with bewilderment. Her knowledge of reading was primitive and the cursive script told her nothing.

'Cyrus B Sedgewick,' the stranger explained grandly as he came to her rescue. 'Representative of Sedgewick, Smith and Sedgewick, of Cheyenne City, Wyoming.'

'Cheyenne City! My, you are a travellin' man!' Ma Riley gasped in awe.

She eyed the luggage and particularly noted the wooden structure sticking out at each end of the leather bag that was now being carried up the stairs by the surly bartender.

'Would you be one of them photographic gentlemen?' she asked.

'Photographic?'

Mr Sedgewick seemed surprised until he noticed the direction of her glance.

'Oh, no, ma'am,' he answered cheerfully. 'That is the tripod of a scientific instrument. I am here in Benson's Butte' — he looked round carefully as he lowered his voice — 'on government work. Very important government work.'

'Landsakes! Do you mean that you actually work for the territory legislature?'

Mr Sedgewick looked slightly affronted. 'Indeed, no, ma'am,' he corrected her. 'My company has the honour of being employed by the Government of the United States of America, Washington

DC. We are engaged in making a survey of the county in order to produce better maps for the day when this territory becomes a State of the Union. Very important work, ma'am.'

'Indeedy, yes.'

They were walking up the stairs now, Mr Sedgewick gallantly offering his arm to Ma Riley who took it automatically. His room was the best in the house, overlooking the rear of the building and containing a large bed with faded red hangings. There was a stove by the window that was clean and ready for lighting. A red wool carpet occupied the centre of the floor and a small rosewood mirror shone brightly above the washstand. Mr Sedgewick expressed his satisfaction and was finally left alone to unpack his belongings.

He did this with great care, laying out his possessions neatly in the top drawer of the chest that stood under the window. His razor, mug, and soap were lined up on the washstand and his spare pair of boots sat tidily at the side of the bed. He checked everything carefully, remembering the exact position of each item, smiling to himself as he unpacked the second leather bag. This contained the wooden tripod that had intrigued Ma Riley and everyone else who had seen it. He laid it in the bottom of the wardrobe and then unpacked a polished wooden case of brass-inlaid mahogany that bore his company's name on a gilded label.

It contained a theodolite; a sleek brass instrument that was carefully wrapped in a soft white cloth as it lay on a bed of blue-quilted lining that held it snugly and secure. He checked to make sure that no damage had been done during transit, removing the leather cap from the eyepiece to be absolutely certain. Visibly relieved that a long journey on the roof of a stagecoach had done it no harm, he repacked the instrument and laid it to rest in the wardrobe alongside the tripod. The last items out of the second bag were two well-worn, fat, leather cases. One was an official map case as used by the military in the late war. He laid them beside the theodolite and closed the wardrobe door.

His work done, Mr Sedgewick washed himself, combed his hair and, after a check in the mirror, went out for a walk to inspect the town of Benson's Butte. He noted the position of the livery stable, the smithy, the marshal's office and the bank. His sharp grey eyes missed nothing of importance and, when he returned to the saloon for something to eat, he was a satisfied man.

It was late in the afternoon when he emerged into the street again. He walked slowly along, his thumbs hooked into waistcoat pockets and the heavy gold watch chain prominently displayed across his broad torso. The bank was a small place, rather bare and with one plain counter dividing the room. It sported two large pewter inkwells and a couple of worn pens on sheets of blotting paper. There was no safe visible, but the far wall bore a frosted glass door that led to some inner sanctum.

A solitary clerk of advanced years looked up from a column of figures when Mr Sedgewick entered. His old eyes opened a little wider at seeing the sort of customer now rather scarce in Benson's Butte. He hitched up his green linen cuffs a little higher and managed an ingratiating smile.

'Good mornin', sir. How can I help you?' he asked, in a reedy voice.

Mr Sedgewick felt in the side pocket of his coat and produced a long envelope.

'My name is Sedgewick,' he said grandly, 'and I have a draft on your bank for two hundred dollars, I believe. Forwarded by the company of Sedgewick, Smith and Sedgewick, of Cheyenne, through Taylor's Banking House.'

'Yes, sir . . . I'll check right away.'

The clerk scurried through the door to the rear while Mr Sedgewick calmly looked around. There was a fine layer of dust over everything and an air of defeat that he had noticed around the town on his earlier walk.

The banker himself came hurrying through the door of the inner sanctum. He was a little man, but held himself erect with an air of pomposity aided by a high celluloid collar and large cravat that held a diamond pin. He wore long sideburns and a small moustache and beard. His head was almost totally bald but great tufts of white hair covered each ear. He had alert eyes above a hawk-like nose and smiled his welcome.

'My dear sir, I've been expecting you,' he said warmly, as he opened a flap in the counter to admit the visitor. He ushered Mr Sedgewick into his private office and offered him a chair in front of the small desk. The surveyor sat down and his keen glance noted the large safe in the far wall with the generous supply of whiskey bottles on top of it. The lit stove was making the room over-warm while blue curtains

shrouding the window made it necessary for an oil lamp to be lit on the desk
even in daytime.

'My name is Hackman, sir,' the
banker said, as he took down one of the
bottles and raised an eyebrow in
invitation. 'The draft got here on last
month's stage and I was wondering
when you were going to arrive. We're
very isolated, as you can see.'

'Indeed you are, sir,' Mr Sedgewick
agreed as he took the whiskey and
tasted it. The quality was good and he
sat back contentedly in his chair.

'Would you like the cash in notes or
gold?'

The surveyor did not answer for a
moment; he appeared to be giving the
matter his earnest judgement.

'I don't really want all the money at
once,' he said slowly, 'so perhaps
twenty dollars in bills would do for
now. I can draw on the rest as needed.
I have some cash on me, of course,
but the company felt it best that I
shouldn't carry too much on a long

journey. One has to be careful.'

The banker nodded eagerly. 'Quite right. Quite right. We haven't had a hold-up for a couple of years, but the less money carried on a journey, the better. After all, that's what banks are for.'

Mr Hackman picked up the letter of credit that the surveyor had given to the clerk, and placed it in an envelope with the original order that he'd received from Cheyenne. He crossed to the safe and brought out some new five-dollar bills that he counted out carefully on to the desk.

'There you are, sir, and a pleasure to do business with your company. If you'll just sign here . . . '

Mr Sedgewick obliged and made to stand up and leave. The banker apparently had other plans. He sat down again and leaned forward eagerly in his chair.

'Tell me, sir,' he said confidentially, 'what is happening about statehood? We get news so slowly here and there was nothing in the mail that came on the stage today. It was most unrewarding.'

They spoke for a while about events in the legislature and the politics of the region. Mr Sedgewick was well informed and the banker listened with rapt attention.

'And . . . er . . . your interest in our town, sir?' he prompted.

It was the surveyor's turn to lean forward confidentially.

'Well, now,' he said carefully, 'the Government in Washington seems quite certain that we'll have statehood in the next year or so. My company has, therefore, been employed to survey parts of the territory wherever they think the maps are too meagre. Did you know that at least three towns are not on the current maps at all? That may do for a territory where everybody knows these places, but it won't do for a State of the Union. My guess . . . and it's only a guess . . . is that there'll be money available in the next few years for better roads and the extension of the telegraph.'

The banker sighed heavily. 'We could certainly use the telegraph,' he admitted, 'and the railroad would be a gift from the Almighty. Have we any hopes in that direction?'

Mr Sedgewick did not answer at once. He looked a little disconcerted, as if he had already said too much or had wandered into deep water.

'As to that . . . ' — he spread his hands in disclaimer — 'I naturally cannot answer. These are matters for the people in Washington circles.'

'Of course. Of course.'

Mr Sedgewick left shortly afterwards and the banker sat thoughtfully at his desk, drumming his stubby fingers uneasily on the worn blotter. He picked up the envelope containing the bank draft to read through both documents again. Arriving at a decision, he took up his hat and left the bank after telling the clerk that if anything urgent cropped up, he would be at Ma Riley's place.

He hurried along the sidewalk in jerky little steps, saluting those citizens he passed who were worthy of his condescension. The saloon was reasonably empty and, after nodding to the owner, he looked around for the man he wanted.

His quarry was a withered-looking fellow who could have been in his late sixties or seventies and who didn't seem to have shaved for the last few weeks. He wore old pants, a thick check shirt that was several sizes too big for him and was leaning against the bar with a whiskey glass in his hand. His washed-out eyes gazed unseeingly at the mirror in front of him.

'Like to earn a little cash, Cy?' the banker murmured in his ear.

The old soak looked at the newcomer with an expression that was more alert than might have been expected.

'How much?' he asked bluntly.

'Two dollars . . . for now.'

'If killin' is what you have in mind, I don't shoot so good these days.'

The banker smiled a little primly at the joke.

'Did you see the man who arrived on today's stage?' he asked.

'Sure did. Fancy dresser from the big city. Another moneylender like yourself, I was thinkin'.'

'I am a banker.'

'If you say so, Mr Hackman. I saw him.'

'I want you to keep an eye on the man and tell me everything he does and everyone he sees around town.'

'For how long? That could be a mighty big two dollars' worth of lookin'.'

'Just until we know what his game is. You can't trust these city folk.'

The old drinker nodded and pushed his now empty glass in front of the banker. Mr Hackman was forced to take the hint and ordered him another whiskey before joining Ma Riley at the far end of the bar.

'You don't often darken my doorstep, Gil,' she greeted him warmly. 'You seem to do all your drinkin' very private-like these days.'

He laid one of his warm hands on her arm.

'A banker must be discreet, my dear lady,' he said softly. 'An example of family virtue and the pillar of rectitude.'

She laughed; a surprisingly melodious noise that travelled round the room.

'Rectitude! Now, that's a fancy word for an old roustabout who chased a naked whore all over this building on Christmas Eve a few years back.'

He flushed angrily. 'The bitch had stolen my watch!' he protested.

'You could have at least put your pants on instead of showin' us all your pillar of rectitude.'

He managed a slight smile at the memory. 'Well, it was a long time ago and we'd all had a few drinks that night. No harm was done.' He squeezed her hand. 'You're more interesting than any of those young girls you employ, Ma. You're a fine figure of a woman.'

She withdrew her hand gently. 'I don't sell what I've got, and you're after something right now,' she said, 'so let's get down to business. What's goin' on around here, Gil?'

'Tell me about Sedgewick.'

She gave the banker a long, steady look before answering.

'He came in on the stage,' she said slowly, 'and booked into my best room for a week or two. Nothin' very definite, but he says he's got important work to do for the Government in Washington. Washington, no less!'

'Where is he now?'

'I think he went out about half an hour ago . . .'

Hackman tapped with his signet ring on the bar to attract Cy's attention. The old man looked up from his drink and the banker called him over.

'He's still around town, Cy,' he muttered. 'Go follow him and make sure he doesn't know he's being watched.'

The old man reluctantly finished his drink and shuffled out of the saloon.

'This must be important,' Ma Riley said musingly. 'Cy doesn't give up his drinkin' for nothin', and you don't go throwin' money around just to be kind to the old folk. Come on, Gil Hackman, what's happenin'?'

'Nothing's happening, so don't try building something out of burnt straw. It's just that this fellow has arrived out of the blue and I've been sent a bank transfer of money for his use here in town. He's supposed to be doing a mapping survey for Washington. It may all be true, but I have a feeling . . .'

'Yes?'

'There's been a parcel of talk about the Homestead Act recently. A lot of the ranchers don't have title to the land they use. They came to the territory after the Act was enforced. Only a few of the early settler families like the Bensons have title to a decent acreage. If he's surveying out here, it could have something to do with more sheep coming in, or more settlers. We need to know enough to protect ourselves.'

Ma Riley poured out a couple of drinks from a special bottle that was kept for her friends.

'We don't want sheep,' she said firmly. 'They've caused enough trouble up north.'

'Exactly, and we don't want any more settlers. The grass won't support the cattle we've got now. The only thing we need round here is a railroad, and that's the last thing we're likely to get. Funnily enough though, he got a bit flustered when I mentioned the railroad. We've got to know more about him, Ma.'

She nodded agreement. 'How can I help?'

'I need to see any papers he's carrying, and I want to know what's in his luggage.'

Ma Riley smiled a serene, self-satisfied smile. Gil Hackman placed his hand upon her arm again and squeezed. He had not misjudged the owner of the saloon.

'You're a sly one, Ma,' he said. 'What did you find?'

She shrugged. 'Nothing I could see

that was important,' she admitted. 'Good quality clothes and boots. Handsome-made shirts from the East, and some real Havana cigars in a leather case.'

The banker looked disappointed. 'Nothing else?' he asked.

'Some instrument.'

'Surveying instrument perhaps.'

'Yes, that's a word he used. He gave it some fancy name when I thought he was one of them photographic men.'

'Theodolite?'

'Sounds like it. Real fancy it is, in a wooden box all wrapped up in a cloth like a new-born babe. Then there's the three-legged thing to set it on, and two leather cases with maps and papers.'

Hackman's grip tightened on her arm. 'That's it,' he murmured.

'That's what?'

'The map cases contain all the information about his work. We've got to see inside them.'

'I saw inside. Just a few maps of the county and a book full of figurin', but I haven't enough readin' to know what it was all about.'

'It doesn't matter, Ma. I can do all the reading. Was there anything else?'

'There was a length of chain in one of them map cases. Why should a man carry a chain with him?'

'It's a measuring chain. Surveyors use them in their work. So, we at least know that he's doing a survey, but we need to know why. When he's out of the way and we know he won't be back for some time, I've got to get in that room and look at those papers. Any sign of a gun?'

'No, unless he's carrying it with him.'

As Ma Riley poured another drop of her good whiskey, the saloon doors opened and Mr Sedgewick entered with his confident, bouncy tread. He was carrying a clean sack that was about half full of something soft and not very heavy. He saluted the owner and the banker before going upstairs to the privacy of his room. They watched until he was out of sight.

'I wonder where he's been,' Ma Riley mused.

'We'll soon know. Cy should be on his trail.'

The old drunk shuffled into the saloon a few minutes later. He went to his usual place at the counter and ordered a beer. Mr Hackman waited impatiently for him to slake the dust from his throat and make a casual move along the bar to where Ma and the banker were standing.

'Well?' Hackman pressed him urgently.

'He went down to Macy and got hisself a ridin' horse and saddle. Paid ready cash for a week's hire. Then he went to Bligget's store and outfitted himself with some clothes more suitable for a horse than that fancy get-up he's wearin' now. Even bought hisself a dandy pair of spurs. Right dude types.'

'And that's what he was carrying in the sack?'

'Sure was,' the old man nodded. 'Bought some tin plates and cups too.

Like he was thinkin' of campin'-out someplace.'

'Did he buy a gun?'

'Nope.'

'If he's going to move around, he's going to need one, if only for rattlers.'

'We ain't got many rattlers round here. Leastways, I've never seen one. I seen other things, though.'

'I can imagine. Is that the lot?'

The old man put his head on one side in passable imitation of a wise and ancient owl.

'I reckon that's a good two dollars' worth of followin',' he said, holding out a grimy hand.

The banker hesitated and then reluctantly took a couple of silver coins from the pocket of his waistcoat. He looked at them as though in mourning before passing them silently across. Cy spat on them enthusiastically, winked at a smiling Ma Riley, and tucked them away in the pocket of his shirt.

'He did make one more call,' he said slyly.

'Yes?'

The old man swallowed the rest of his beer and put the glass down on the counter as he licked his lips. Ma Riley nodded to the bartender to refill it.

'Yes?' Mr Hackman tried again.

'He did a mighty odd thing for a stranger in town,' old Cy volunteered between large gulps.

'And what would that be?' the banker snapped impatiently.

'He called at the funeral parlour.'

4

Ma Riley and the banker looked at each other in surprise.

'What would he be doing at the funeral parlour?' Hackman asked in bewilderment. 'There haven't been any deaths in town.'

The elderly drunk knew that he had his audience and he moved closer to give them the benefit of his alcoholic breath.

'He wanted something made of wood, I reckon,' he said.

'And what did he want made?'

Hackman was impatient and Cy realized that this was not the time to play the fool.

'Well,' he said, 'he weren't in there very long and I think Jeff Bishop must have sent him to the carpentry shop. The dude wanted some poles makin'. Six feet long and with black and white stripes down 'em. Didn't seem to make no sense to me.'

'It makes sense all right,' Hackman snapped. 'He was just ordering measuring poles. My own intelligence should have told me he wouldn't carry things like that on the stage. It just confirms that he's doing survey work. That was a good job you did, Cy.'

'I could still keep an eye on him,' the old man suggested.

'Why not? It can't do any harm.'

Cy went back to his own favourite part of the bar and paid for his next drink out of one of the new silver dollars.

It was an hour or more before Mr Sedgewick came downstairs again and walked sedately in the direction of the marshal's office. It was also the jailhouse, a sturdy wooden building with small windows and a solid door.

Matt Sawyer was seated behind his desk and looked up in surprise from the magazine he was reading. The surveyor introduced himself and the two men shook hands. Mr Sedgewick was waved to one of the rickety chairs.

'And what can I do for you, sir?' the marshal asked.

'I am in need of a little advice from a man in authority,' the visitor explained. 'My job is to survey this area of Wyoming on behalf of the Government of the United States, and I have need of an assistant. Nothing very special, but a man who can do some plain cooking, guard me and my equipment out in the field and generally make himself useful. A sound man with a horse and gun, you understand.'

'Sure, I get your point,' the marshal said, 'but there ain't many men in town who answer that description. Those who lost their jobs on the cattle spreads have already moved on, and the regular townfolk have full-time work.'

'I saw an old-timer in Ma Riley's place. He didn't seem to be working and I wondered if he could be recommended. I think his name was Cy.'

The marshal laughed at the idea.

'Old Cy!' he spluttered. 'He's the town drunk. No, he can run a few errands and chop wood for widow women, but that's about his limit. He ain't even got a horse no more, and that old Navy Colt is apt to fire off all the chambers at once. He don't clean it too good.'

'Well, thanks for the warning, Marshal.'

Matt Sawyer thought about the problem for a moment or two.

'There is one young fella,' he said slowly. 'He drifted into town a couple of days back. He's a cowpoke lookin' for work. He can certainly handle himself, though he ain't got a gun; sold it to eat.'

'I could buy a gun on expenses, that's no problem. But can he be trusted?'

The marshal scratched his head. 'Well, now, he seems a decent fella and I've offered him a deputy's job. I haven't checked his background because he ain't accepted yet, but if he works with you for a while, it'll give him time to make up his mind about settlin' down here.'

'It would certainly help both of us,' the surveyor agreed. 'Where will I find him?'

'I reckon he might be takin' a drink at Ma's place. Everyone ends up there sooner or later.'

'I've just left there. What does he look like?'

The marshal got up and crossed to one of the windows.

'Oh, he's about medium height, a bit scrawny, biggish nose, dark-brown eyes, slicked hair, and he's dressed in an old blue shirt.'

'That's an impressive description, Marshal,' Mr Sedgewick said admiringly. 'Goes with the job, I suppose.'

'Not really. I'm just watchin' him come along the street. He's turnin' into Ma's place at this very minute.'

The two men laughed and the surveyor left the office to catch up with Bill Quince. The cowpoke was at the bar counting out small change for a glass of beer.

'Let me buy that,' Mr Sedgewick intervened.

He received a blank and slightly hostile stare.

'I can buy my own drinks, mister,' Bill Quince said bleakly.

'No offence intended, but I've just been speaking to the marshal and it's possible that you and I can help each other.'

'Yeah?'

Old Cy edged nearer to hear what was being said and listened avidly as Mr Sedgewick told the cowpoke of his need for an assistant. Quince gradually smiled and put the coins away in his shirt pocket.

'Well, I reckon you can buy me that drink after all,' he said. 'I'll have a whiskey with a beer chaser.'

Cy chuckled. He liked a man with a bit of style.

The drinks were produced as the two men talked. While Quince remained at the bar, the surveyor finally went up to his room. Cy swallowed his drink and hurried off to report to the banker.

Marshal Sawyer watched him scurrying down the main street, holding on to his felt hat with one hand and steadying the Navy Colt with the other. The marshal picked up his own hat and left the office. He crossed to the hardware store and waited until fat old Harry had served his customer.

'What can I do for you, Marshal?' Harry wheezed, as he settled his bulk on the barrel he used as a seat.

'Would your lad be goin' into Little Bear this week?'

'Sure. Tomorrow, like as not. We need a few things if they've been freighted from Underwood.'

The marshal shook his head. 'Sure is a round-about way we have of doin' business in this town,' he said ruefully.

'That it is, and I reckon it'll last my lifetime. Rail from Cheyenne to Underwood, freight from there to Little Bear, and then at least two days to get to Benson's Butte. One hell of a way to run a town. Now, what can I do for you, Matt?'

'I'd be obliged if your boy could deliver some messages for me in Little Bear. One to the marshal and another to the telegraph office. It's official business and I'd be right grateful.'

'I'll send him to the jailhouse first thing in the morning.'

'Much obliged, Harry.'

The marshal took his leave and went to another store where he leaned over the glass-topped counter that held a small display of guns.

'I got a question for you, Bill,' he said to the owner, 'but I don't need the answer till tomorrow.'

★　★　★

The next morning was dry and a slight wind blew up the dust as Mr Sedgewick and Quince steered their horses out of the smithy corral and headed for open country. They carried the surveying gear and the city man was plainly dressed in a wool shirt and serge pants.

The cowpoke now carried a gun. It was a worn .45 Colt in an old holster with plenty of spare ammunition in a broad belt.

The marshal watched from his office. When the two riders moved out of his range of vision, he went across to the store where the owner was sweeping out.

'What's the answer to my question, Bill?' he asked.

'It ain't the one I'd wish it to be,' the man answered. 'I like to make me a profit.'

★　★　★

Quince and the surveyor rode in a companionable silence. Their horses' hooves threw up a haze of pale dust and the sun was getting warmer as it rose in the sky and pushed the mist away from the butte. A single buzzard watched the scene from a rocky outcrop and then flew off as the men approached. Bill Quince's body tensed, and his head moved jerkily from side to side. The surveyor noticed his agitation.

'What's worrying you?' he asked.

'I don't know, and that's what's worrying me. That buzzard wasn't spooked by us.'

He moved the clip from the top of the holstered gun and, as he did so, a shot rang out and Bill Quince pitched from his horse to land face down in a patch of low bushes.

5

The thing was so sudden that Sedgewick sat glued in his saddle, trying to control his horse. Quince was crawling along the ground, gun in hand and hugging the dirt.

'Get down here!' he shouted. 'The bastard might not miss with the next shot.'

Sedgewick slipped hurriedly to the ground and doubled for cover behind the rocks. The cowpoke joined him there while their horses wandered down the trail in the direction of town.

'Someone's after us,' Quince whispered. 'You've made enemies in Benson's Butte.'

'It's more likely to be that Pete fellow you had trouble with. He shot at you, not me.'

'It could just be that he wasn't shootin' at either of us. I might be wrong but I reckon he was aimin' to miss.'

'Then what the hell is he playing at?' Sedgewick asked peevishly.

Quince sneaked a look round the edge of a boulder. There was no movement from the opposite clump of bushes. He took aim and fired a single shot into the clump.

'Did you hit him?' Sedgewick asked.

'I didn't even see him. Just wanted him to know we have him pinned down.'

'How do you figure that out? He's bushwhacked us, as I see it.'

'He's stuck there without a horse, same as we are. There's no animal nearby and he's trapped. A real careless *hombre*.'

Sedgewick licked his lips nervously. 'Then he isn't a professional?' he asked hopefully.

'It ain't likely. He's using a shotgun and he must have aimed wild. I only got one pellet in the left arm and he could have given me a full barrel at that range. It's all a big screwy.'

'What should we do then?'

'Play it safe and wait here. I'll get him as soon as he makes a move.'

'It might take hours,' the surveyor murmured anxiously.

'We outwait him. He's got at least one more barrelful of buckshot and he might aim closer next time.'

'I see your point. We'll wait.'

The two men lay silently on the ground, Mr Sedgewick sweating, while the cowpoke watched the bushes on the other side of the trail. A small lizard crawled across the rocks and scampered off when the surveyor moved his cramped leg.

'Somebody's comin',' Quince said quietly. 'Look back there.'

There was a haze of dust between them and the town and a lone horseman was travelling towards them at a steady pace.

'I wonder whose side he's on,' Quince mused as he cocked his pistol.

It was Marshal Sawyer, his left hand controlling the reins of a large bay gelding, while his right led two riderless horses, which the crouching men recognised as belonging to them. He stopped about forty feet away and raised himself in the saddle to view the area better.

'Cy!' he bellowed angrily. 'Get your scraggy ass out from that scrub before I pepper it with buckshot.'

There was a long pause before the bent figure of an old man appeared carrying a large jack-rabbit.

'I ain't done no harm, Marshal,' he protested. 'Just gettin' a bit of meat for my dinner.'

'Come here, you silly old goat.'

While Sedgewick and his assistant got to their feet, the old man wandered across to the marshal and proudly displayed the jack-rabbit.

'I didn't mean to spook no one,' he said penitently, 'but they just happened along as I let fly.'

'Get the hell outa here,' the marshal ordered. 'You might have killed someone. I should throw you into jail for bein' drunk.'

The old man scrambled away, muttering apologies to the men he had scared. They approached the marshal to offer their thanks for his timely appearance.

'I saw him leavin' town just before you,' Matt Sawyer explained, 'and when I heard a shotgun go off and then a pistol, I got me a mite anxious. I was at the edge of town by then and your horses came trottin' in.'

'I thought we was bein' bushwhacked,' Quince said. 'He might have got hisself shot if you'd not come along.'

'That's what I reckoned,' the marshal agreed. 'I see you got yourself a gun. Know how to use it?'

'I manage.'

'Well, I'll leave you folks to go about your business and I'll be about mine.'

The marshal handed over the reins of the horses and turned his own mount back towards town. Quince and the surveyor mounted up.

'Too smooth,' Quince said, as they rode off.

'What do you mean?'

'That old soak left town on foot just a few minutes before us. He planted himself in that clump of bushes and, as we was passin', he shoots himself a jack-rabbit.'

'I suppose it could happen that way.'

'No, it couldn't. That clump of bushes ain't more than nine feet across. We'd have seen him if he'd been after jack-rabbits, and the one he said he shot would have had to be a sight further from him than the ground covered by them bushes. It looked stiff enough to have been shot last night.'

'So you think he was shooting at us then?' Sedgewick asked.

'No, I think he was spyin'. He probably moved awkward-like and the gun went off. Gave hisself away.'

'He couldn't hope to follow us very far on foot.'

'Just far enough to make sure we was outa town.'

'And what about the marshal?'

'I reckon he's watchin' everyone,' Quince grinned. 'Lawmen are just naturally curious.'

* * *

The marshal soon caught up with the shuffling old drunk and slowed his horse to keep pace with him.

'You were a mite lucky back there, Cy. That Quince fella could have filled you with a lotta lead.'

'It was just an accident, Marshal, honest, it was . . . '

'Those folks ain't stupid, you old fool. What in hell's name were you up to?'

'Honest, Marshal . . . '

The lawman reined in his horse. 'I'll tell you how it is, Cy. You can go to jail for bein' drunk as a skunk, or you can tell me what it's all about.'

The old man thought it over and eyed the marshal craftily.

'Well, I reckon you're a better cook than I am,' he said, 'so maybe a few days in jail would do my old bones good . . . '

'We only serve coffee in the jailhouse, Cy. There's no whiskey or beer.'

'Jesus, Marshal! You're a hard man.'

★　★　★

Gil Hackman was at the bank when Cy made his report. He did not mention falling over, discharging the gun, or being made to talk by the marshal. He knew when to be discreet.

The banker gave him a silver dollar and was at the saloon a few minutes later, walking up the back stairs with Ma Riley. She opened up Sedgewick's room and the two of them began searching. It was the broadcloth coat that gave the only valuable information. In one of the pockets was a new-looking visiting card.

'This is what we want,' the banker said eagerly. 'It belongs to a manager of the railroad. He's obviously working in cahoots with Sedgewick and they're surveying land to lay rails. We've hit pay-dirt, Ma.'

Ma Riley sat on the edge of the bed, her brow wrinkled.

'What will it really mean to us?' she asked.

He sat down beside her and took a warm, moist hand in his.

'If the railroad comes through Benson's Butte, the ranchers will bring their cattle into town and get them to the markets much faster. They won't have to spend days on the trail. Then there would be more visitors to town, more money all round, and better times for everyone. The telegraph would follow and we'd really be on the map. The good days would be here again.'

He looked round the room to make sure that everything was in order.

'We've got to make another search when he's having dinner. I must see what's in his map cases.'

Ma Riley nodded her understanding, but her face wore an anxious look.

'I'm scared of all this, Gil,' she admitted.

He hugged her. 'Don't be, Ma. I know what I'm doing and you and I are going to come out of this affair mighty rich folks.'

6

Mr Hackman was unable to search Sedgewick's room again that evening. The surveyor returned late to town, slept for a while, and then only went down to the bar for a quiet drink before returning to rest.

It was the following night that things happened. Sedgewick was in a hungrier mood, changed into his city suit, sat down to a large dinner and then played poker with three of the townsmen. Ma Riley and the banker sneaked into his room and removed the leather map cases from the wardrobe. Hackman spread out the maps on the bed while Ma held the lamp close.

'Here it is,' the banker whispered excitedly. 'This thick line is the rail route from Cheyenne through the territory. And see that dotted line? That's the proposed route.'

'How much nearer is it to us?' the woman asked.

'I'd need a rule to measure it correctly, but I'd guess we're talking about fifteen miles from here. Maybe twenty.'

'Is that any good?'

'Not unless the train stops. He's surveyed as far as Still Creek and you can see the way he's following the water supply.'

'We got plenty of water here in town.'

'Yes, but they also have to consider the lay of the land. We've got to persuade this fellow that it would be better to put the rails through Benson's Butte.'

Ma Riley frowned and her little mouth grew even smaller in a worried pout. The banker was examining some notebooks.

'This is useless,' he said bitterly. 'They don't seem to be planning any sort of stop between here and Chugwater. This layout won't help us at all.'

'Well, at least he's not workin' for

homesteaders or sheep men.'

'That's small consolation.'

He put the maps away and made sure that the room looked undisturbed.

'What now?' Ma asked, when they were in the corridor.

'Let's go to your room.'

'I'm not in the mood for that.'

'Neither am I,' the banker snapped. 'I need time to think things over. Go and see if Cy is in the bar. If he is, send him up to me.'

Ma Riley did as she was told and Gil Hackman installed himself in her comfortable room and had a large whiskey while he waited. He had almost dozed off when Cy came through the door without knocking. The old man looked round in wonderment.

'I've got another little job for you, Cy,' the banker told him without preamble. 'You've got to do some travelling.'

The old man's face lit up. 'To Cheyenne City?' he asked hopefully.

'Not that far. Just to the Macready

spread. Tell Jacob to send out messages to George Martin, Sam Benson, and Doug Winfield to meet me there on Thursday afternoon. I'll give you a note in my office first thing in the morning. You can also hire a horse from Macy.'

He put a heavy hand on the man's shoulder. 'This is strictly between you and me, Cy. These ranchers are mean folk and they don't like their affairs being talked of around the town.'

'You can trust me, boss. I don't talk. Not never.'

Mr Hackman was satisfied with his day's work. He had greater ambitions than any he had mentioned to Ma or would mention to the ranchers. He left the saloon to visit the mayor. He and Paul Redding were not close friends but they represented the social backbone of the town. The mayor was a lawyer who had married a rich woman and lived in comfort on the edge of Benson's Butte.

The unexpected visitor was greeted with respect and Mrs Redding went off to make coffee while the men sat down to talk. The mayor was a small man, slighty bowed and with rimless glasses on the edge of his nose. His bald head shone in the lamplight.

'Don't have you calling very often, Gil,' he said warily.

'Well, I'm kept pretty busy, like yourself,' the banker replied. 'The fact is that I've been doing some thinking about how bad things are in town. The time's come to do something about it.'

'Indeed?'

'I reckon that Benson's Butte has to have the railroad and the telegraph. We need those two things if the town is to survive.'

'I agree, but there's no chance. We're a back-water now . . . '

'Not if you have a friend in the right place. The man of the hour, so to speak.'

'Man of the hour?'

'I've been putting our case to Cheyenne,' Hackman explained without a blush, 'and I know a lot of folks in the legislature and on the board of the railroad. It hasn't been easy, but my work is beginning to bear fruit. There's a surveyor in town, following my suggestion to the right parties. He's mapping out a route. It's not quite what we want, but I'm still working on it. I'm putting a scheme to the cattle men that should get us a halt for freight and passengers. I might even get them to bring the rails right through town. I thought you ought to know as soon as possible. I didn't speak sooner because I couldn't be sure of pulling it off.'

The mayor was all agog. 'Can I help in any way?' he asked.

'Not at the moment, Paul. But suppose . . . just suppose that I manage to make it come about, what then?'

'Gil, this town would be eternally grateful. They might even put up a statue to you.'

Hackman tried to look modest. 'Sounds fine,' he said quietly. 'Right fine. But statues usually come after you're dead. I was thinking of something to enjoy while I'm still alive.'

The mayor looked puzzled for a moment. Then frowned.

'Do you mean a public subscription?' he asked coldly.

'Hell, no! Money's the last thing on my mind. No Paul, I was thinking of going into politics. I'd like a seat in the legislature.'

The mayor visibly relaxed. 'And you want my help?' he asked. 'Gil, nothing would please me more. The whole town would be behind you. Of course, the legislature might be near its end. There's all this talk of statehood.'

Gil Hackman nodded his agreement. The mayor had walked into the trap.

'It's only a matter of time,' he said firmly. 'A year or so at the most. And then I'll need all the local support I can muster to get into the Congress of the United States of America.'

7

Cy was not in Ma Riley's the next day but Macy told the marshal that he'd rented him a horse and the old man had ridden out of town early in the morning. Matt Sawyer guessed that the drunk was on some errand for Gil Hackman.

Hackman himself rode out on Thursday morning. The marshal shook his head in puzzlement. He could not get rid of the feeling that something was happening under his nose and that he was the only one not to know what it was.

The banker arrived at the Macready ranch in the early afternoon. He was not a good horseman, but had travelled as quickly as possible. The Macready spread was one of the newer ones and the house was well built and freshly painted. Jacob came to the edge of the porch to welcome his visitor. He was a large man, in his late fifties and with a face battered by the weather. He led Hackman into a long room that had walls of pale wood adorned with the heads of deer.

The other ranchers were already there, smoking cigars and filling the air with the fragrance of tobacco. There was George Martin, wiry and in his forties; next to him was the senior rancher. He stood out from the others because of his black suit and stock that made him look like a preacher-man. He had a long, discontented face fringed with a beard in the fashion of the late Abe Lincoln. His mouth was turned down at the corners and he was the only one without a whiskey glass at his elbow. He was Sam Benson, the ageing son of the earliest settler who had founded Benson's Butte.

Across from him was Doug Winfield. He was a stout and jolly man whose looks hid a hard determination to get all he wanted out of life. His smooth, pleasant face was wreathed in smiles as he greeted the banker.

Gil Hackman thanked them for assembling and began to tell them all he felt they should know about the survey. They listened in silence, just nodding now and then as they agreed with his diagnosis.

'So you can see, gentlemen,' he ended, 'that we have got to get the rails as near town as possible with a halt for freight. This is a matter of great urgency.'

'What's in it for you, Gil?' one of them asked.

'A bank needs a prosperous town. Everybody gains if we have the railroad and telegraph.'

Doug Winfield leaned forward. 'If this fella's plannin' to go north of town,' he asked, 'what can we do about it?'

'Persuade him,' Hackman said.

'You mean that we bribe the bastard?' George Martin grunted.

'We show him where his best interests lie,' Hackman replied.

'So what sort of money are we talkin' about?' Macready asked.

'I think we should have a pool of cash we can draw on. About a thousand dollars apiece. Five thousand in all. Then we can negotiate and get the best deal we can.'

'I'd go aong with that,' Martin said.

'So would I,' Macready agreed, 'but we'd have to hold back until we were absolutely sure. I won't invest a thousand dollars in anyone's good faith.'

Hackman nodded. 'I'll put it to him that we're prepared to supply a reasonable fee if he sees our point of view. Some cash on the barrel and the rest when construction actually starts.'

'Once work starts,' Doug Winfield said with a cherubic grin, 'Mister City Slicker Surveyor can go piss in the creek for the balance.'

There was a burst of laughter and the whiskey bottle went round. One of the men coughed loudly and all eyes turned on Sam Benson. He sat in funereal gloom.

'What's your view, Sam?' Jacob Macready asked hastily.

The senior rancher rose like an Old Testament prophet.

'I have heard men talkin' here,' he said in a deeply resonant voice, 'of things that are of the vileness of greed. God tells me that you are all in grievous error and will answer for it on the Day of Judgement. Bribery is an act of baseness and I will have naught to do with it. I shall pray for your souls, brothers, and I wish you a good day.'

He stalked to the door and turned for a final shot.

'God speaks through me!' he roared. 'And my words are the words of the Lord.'

They sat in silence until the clatter of his horse was heard leaving the yard. Then there was a bellow of laughter and another round of drinks.

Gil Hackman rode back to town content enough with the day's work.

Sam Benson's defection did not matter. The rest of them could do a deal with the surveyor that would profit everyone.

★   ★   ★

Saturday night in Benson's Butte started off as quietly as usual. Ma's saloon was brightly lit and it was nearly ten in the evening when the first of the ranch hands began to drift into town. They came in twos and threes until about fifteen horses were tied up at the hitching rail. The men stood at the bar, drinking steadily and getting noisier as the liquor got to them.

Mr Sedgewick sat at a table with the banker. They were drinking whiskey and making polite conversation. Hackman was going along with the pretence that the surveyor was map-making. The noise at the bar became more intrusive. Two of the cowpokes were pushing at each other and shouting drunkenly. Ma Riley came down the stairs and went across to them.

'Cut that ruckus!' she shrieked. 'If any son of a bitch wants a fight, he can start by fightin' me!'

That was usually enough to restore order. Ma had a hard fist, pointed boots, and a derringer in the pocket of her skirt. The ranch hands gave way before her but seemed to close in again. Two more of them started pushing each other and somebody threw a bottle that smashed the gilt wall mirror. Ma Riley screamed in rage as the bartenders reached for the pick-axe handles they used as a first line of defence.

A shot rang out and all the regulars headed for the door or ducked under the tables. Mr Sedgewick and the banker joined them and turned white, frightened faces to one another.

'This hasn't happened for years,' Hackman quavered. 'I can't understand it.'

'Are they local men?' Sedgewick asked anxiously.

'From Sam Benson's spread. They

usually behave themselves.'

The shots were flying thick and fast now. Most of them went into the ceiling or through the window. Ma's voice could be heard above the din as she laid about her with clenched fists. Tables were being smashed and a chair was flung across the bar. The bartenders were kept at bay by two men who fired shots over their heads every time they were foolish enough to raise them above the counter. Ma Riley picked up a broken bottle and was getting ready to use it when help arrived.

The marshal stood in the open doorway with a shotgun pointed at the brawlers. There was an almost instant hush as he approached grimly towards the counter. The bartenders slowly rose from their hiding places.

'Collect all the guns,' the marshal told one of them.

He then turned his attention to the fighters, one or two of whom were sneaking out of the door.

'Stay where you are!' he shouted.

'Your horses are no use to you 'cause I've cut the cinches. You can all walk yourselves down to the jailhouse and we'll finish the party there.'

'We was just havin' a bit of fun, Marshal . . . ' one of the men said limply.

'I'm glad to hear that, Ned. I like a bit of fun. Now, start for the jailhouse like a church-school outin'.'

The cowpokes slowly shuffled out of the saloon and along the street to the marshal's office. The bartender followed with a large galvanized bucket full of guns. Matt Sawyer opened up and divided his visitors between the two available cells. He locked the doors and took the bucket off the bartender.

'What the hell were you lot playin' at?' he asked gruffly. 'You're not even liquored up and you wreck Ma's place. What were you supposed to be doin'?'

They stood at the bars, looking hangdog and sullen.

'Mr Benson will have us out in the

mornin', you can bet on that,' Ned Gambley said truculently.

'Will he now? Well, it's goin' to cost him a handful of dollars, that's for sure.'

8

When Bill Quince came out of the barn to wash himself on Sunday morning, he found the marshal making a note of the horses in the corral.

'Mornin', Marshal,' he called out as he dried himelf on a clean floursack.

'Mornin', Bill. Workin' today?'

'Mr Sedgewick likes to lie abed at the weekend,' the cowpoke said cheerfully. 'I got me the day off.'

'Very nice. Is the chore nearly done then?'

'I don't rightly know. He don't tell me nothing. In fact, he don't talk much at all. Maybe he reckons I ain't got the learnin' to make conversation with a man like him.'

'City folk can be like that,' the marshal agreed. 'Did you hear the ruckus at Ma Riley's place last night?'

'Surely got me out of bed when the

shootin' started and things got noisy. I went to watch the fun. You handled it real smooth.'

'I try my best, but they messed up the place mighty bad. I'm just checkin' over their horses in case we have to sell 'em off to pay for the damages. Ma Riley wants two hundred dollars.'

'She sounds a pretty smart lady,' the cowpoke laughed.

'She surely is. Did you see Mr Sedgewick last night?'

'Yeah, I went to Ma's place to make sure he was all right.'

'Was he put out by it?'

'He was some, but I reckon he's seen a few brawls in his travels. He'll get over it.'

'I guess so. See you around, Bill.'

The marshal strolled back up the street and stopped for a moment outside the saloon. The window frames were already being replaced and the damaged furniture was piled in the street. Ma's strident voice could be heard giving orders. A chalked notice on the door told the world that she was still open for business.

The jailhouse smelled a bit strong and the inmates met the marshal with a barrage of complaints. He merely told them to shut up while he settled himself down with the *Diamond Dick* magazine that had come in on the last stage. He enjoyed the Ned Buntline stories, far-fetched though they were, but the print was small and he only read a little at a time.

It was nearly midday when Sam Benson rode into town on his tall bay horse with its elaborate Mexican saddle. He was in black as usual and alighted at the marshal's office with a springy jump that belied his years. Matt Sawyer went out to meet him.

'A warm journey, Sam,' he said by way of greeting.

'As warm as the Almighty wishes it to be.'

'And what can I do for you?'

'I come for my boys,' the rancher said grimly.

'Well, now, your boys have shot up

Ma Riley's saloon and done a lot of damage that has to be paid for. So either they pays or they go up before the judge on Monday mornin'.'

'You ain't got a judge since old Harrington drank hisself to the Devil's embrace.'

'The mayor's taken on the job, and he don't like you, Sam Benson. And he certainly don't like folk shootin' up his town.'

'His town!'

The old rancher's voice rose to a crescendo of indignation.

'My pappy built this town. Gave it his name and chose the first council. He even put up this jailhouse and brought in water from the creek. This ain't the mayor's town: it's Benson's Butte, and don't you forget it. This town was built for God-fearin' folk.'

'I'm glad to hear that, Sam, 'cause your wranglers don't come under that headin'. You'll be mighty pleased we got them in jail, since God-fearin' they ain't.'

'Now, listen to me, you half-blind old buzzard . . . '

'You shouldn't talk to a town marshal like that, Sam. He might not make a deal about that collection of mule droppin's back there. Then how would you run your spread?'

'I've got me enough men . . . '

'Sam, you paid off half your hands, just like the other ranchers. Now, what's it to be? Have them face the judge or swallow your pride and go make peace with Ma?'

'How much does she want?' Sam Benson asked in a calmer voice.

'Two hundred dollars.'

The grim face paled with rage. 'That Whore of Babylon ain't got two hundred dollars'-worth in the whole building. She's bushwhackin' me!'

'Very likely but that's her figure an' I reckon it's cheap at the price. Why not go down and see her?'

'I don't enter the house of the Godless!'

'Use the back door, like you used to

when you paid a monthly call on fat Bella.'

'I was savin' her soul. The Lord spoke to me . . . '

'Sam Benson, you talk a heap of bullshit. Now, let's get down to business: why did you send your men into town to cause all that ruckus?'

There was a long pause and the rancher swallowed noisily.

'Why should I do a thing like that?' he finally asked.

'That was my question, Sam. Your hands wouldn't have dared shoot the place up unless they had your saintly blessing. So, why?'

The rancher blew his nose on a large bandanna.

'Matt,' he said ingratiatingly, 'you and me is old friends . . . we growed up together . . . '

'Me in a sod hut and you in your pappy's fancy ranch.'

'Matt, I got my reasons.'

'So, tell an old friend while he's still friendly.'

Sam Benson came up the shallow steps and leaned against one of the porch supports.

'I gotta take you into my confidence, Matt,' he said quietly. 'I'm goin' to tell you somethin' I wouldn't tell anyone. Not even the family. And I don't want it talked about. Not ever.'

'I never won any medals as the town gossip.'

'All right. I'm a proud man, Matt Sawyer . . .'

'What does the Almighty have to say about pride, Sam? He must be right peeved when you go preachin' at other folks about their sins. I would have thought that pride came pretty high up on the list.'

'You shut your yap, you know-nothin' blasphemer! We're all sinners, and I got my faults same as the next man . . .'

'Well, admittin' them is somethin' I've never heard you do before. Are you learnin' a little humility, Sam?'

'Are you goin' to listen or not?'

'I'm listenin'.'

'Right. Then I'm tellin'. My pappy built this town and he was right proud with what he done and the folks looked up to him. They made him the first mayor. He was mayor for twenty-three years, and when he ascended to the realms of Glory . . . I . . . '

'You hoped the townsfolk would elect you,' the marshal said.

'Yeah, that's the truth of it. And they never did. They picked that skunk-drunk Sam Belling, and when he went to the Devil's Inferno, they chose themselves a lawyer-man! Can you imagine it? A lawyer!'

'Maybe they wanted a good laugh now and then. So, you're mighty put out by the mayors of Benson's Butte? It figures. You reckoned they owed it to you after what your pappy did for the town?'

'That's right.'

'What did you do for the town, Sam?'

The rancher stared angrily. 'What did I do?'

'Yeah. Did you build anythin'? Give

anythin'? By the time your pappy died, you'd got yourself a streak of religion so wide that you couldn't get along with nobody. You quarrelled with just about everyone in Benson's Butte and made yourself as popular as a drunken horsefly. They wouldn't have elected you as a crossin' sweeper.'

'I see things as the Good Lord commands. I am the voice of the Almighty!'

'Sam, as I said before, you talk a lot of bullshit, and I don't reckon the Lord has much to do with it. You're just a bitter old man who hasn't the sense to get under cover when it rains.'

'I ain't been spoken to like that in a hog's age.'

'You should come to town more often. I'm always glad to oblige. So what it amounts to is that you're takin' it out on Ma just because you don't like the way folks treated you in the past. You haven't been in Benson's Butte for ten years at least. So why the sudden interest? And don't start callin' on God again. He's got more on his plate than chattin' to a dried-up old prairie dog like you.'

'It's this railroad.'

The marshal became suddenly alert. 'Railroad?' he muttered.

'Yeah. I don't want no railroad in this town. Not no how.'

Matt Sawyer tried to keep calm. This was the secret he had sensed in the activities around town.

'I should have thought a railroad would have suited you right well, Sam,' he said carefully. 'It'll suit everyone else around here.'

'Matt, I don't want this town to have a railroad or a telegraph. That's my stand and I ain't budgin' from it.'

'That's mighty selfish Sam. You'll make no friends.'

'I got no friends, and I ain't aimin' to be humiliated by the folks of this town no more. They're Godless, and as doomed as the sinners of Sodom and Gomorrah. I want no part of them.'

'And all because they wouldn't vote

for you. You're one hell of a Christian, Sam. So, what has all this got to do with last night?'

'I wanted that surveyor fella to see this as a low-life town and no place for a railroad.'

'That sounds like cuttin' your throat to bleed all over your neighbour's new shirt. If we had rails, you could get your cattle to market quicker and safer. You wouldn't have no worries about pasture, and you'd be in touch by telegraph and know the latest market prices. You're not makin' sense, Sam Benson.'

'It's you that ain't makin' sense, fella. My spread is nearer to Chugwater than anybody else this side of the creek. I save at least three days of travellin' to get a herd to market. If the rails go through Benson's Butte, we're all runnin' equal distance and I got no advantage. Same thing with the telegraph. I'm closer to it than the other ranchers. I can get a rider to send or pick up a message in a few hours.'

'So you get it both ways,' the marshal mused. 'You keep the edge over the other spreads, and you get even with the nasty folk of Benson's Butte.'

'That's about it.'

'You're a beauty, Sam. Go see Ma and settle the account. When you've done that, you can collect your men and their animals.'

The rancher unhitched his horse and mounted.

'Remember Matt Sawyer,' he said, 'what I told you is just between us.'

'You got my word, Sam.'

The rancher nodded stiffly and rode slowly down the street.

'Well, Sam Benson,' the marshal muttered to himself, 'you might not take the prize for Christian charity, but you sure as hell take it for the almightiest liar in Benson's Butte.'

9

It was early Monday morning when Mr Sedgewick stepped out from the saloon and strolled down to the office of Mr Hackman's bank.

'I'd like another fifty dollars from my credit,' he said cheerfully. The clerk nodded eagerly and scurried into the back room to oblige. Mr Hackman emerged a moment or two later and ushered his new-found friend into the inner sanctum. The two men sat on each side of the desk, quietly taking the measure of the other.

'You know, Mr Sedgewick,' the banker said tentatively, 'I'm a man of the world. I notice things. Weigh them up and judge the pros and cons. After all, that's the way we bankers make our money.'

'Quite so,' the surveyor answered politely.

'And this work you're doing . . . I smell something a little more important than map-making.'

'Is that a fact, now?'

'I've got me some pretty good maps of this territory, and I don't see the need of new ones. Not so much that Washington would get involved. I lend money on land and property. You might say that maps are part of my business.'

'I take your point.' The voice was neutral.

'So, what exactly are you surveying, Mr Sedgewick?'

The surveyor was slowly putting away the banknotes and did not appear to hear the question.

'If you're doing what I think you're doing,' the banker went on, 'you'll need local knowledge and banking services. After all, a workforce has to be paid and local store bills settled. This is the nearest bank.'

Sedgewick looked a little disconcerted for a moment.

'Yes,' he said slowly, 'that is a

consideration. Local arrangements will have to be made sooner or later.' He took a deep breath as though making up his mind. 'This is confidential, Hackman,' he said seriously, 'and too early a disclosure could upset things.'

'My lips are sealed, dear friend.'

'Good. Then let's get down to cases. I am surveying for the railroad. They want to run a link to shorten the present route. Construction methods have improved in the last few years and we can clear the ground and lay track faster than in the early days. It could double the number of trains and increase the freight and passenger service enormously.'

'Does this include a route through Benson's Butte?' Mr Hackman asked in an innocent voice.

'No, it will run about fifteen miles north of here. Up near the creek. The ground there is just right and there's plenty of water.'

'I see,' Mr Hackman said slowly. 'So the town will only benefit while the construction work is being done?'

'That's about the long and short of it. Benson's Butte doesn't figure in the company's plans.'

'Yes, but suppose we look at it from another angle: why not bring the rails through town, have a halt here, use our water supply, and help expand Benson's Butte? That would help not only the locals but also the whole territory.'

'Well, the geologists feel that the best route is on the line of the creek, so that's the area I'm surveying. I haven't a very free hand in the matter.'

Hackman rubbed the side of his sweating face.

'Geologists, eh?' he murmured. 'Yes, but could they be wrong? I'm thinking of the winter floods.'

'Floods!' The surveyor looked alarmed.

'Well, of course. You can take it from any local that the creek can rise by three or four feet when the rains come. And we've had some bad winters lately. Real destructive, they've been. Two years back there was nearly a foot of water to within a mile or so of the town. A geologist sitting on his butt in Cheyenne mightn't know about such problems.'

'That could be true,' Mr Sedgewick agreed uncertainly. 'I must confess that flooding was not a consideration. I'd better start looking a bit more to the north . . .'

'And hit the granite outcrops?'

'Granite? Surely not! I didn't know there was any granite round here.'

'All the monuments in the town burial ground are made of it. Bert Rogers is a very classy stonemason.'

Mr Sedgewick rose to leave. 'Well, thank you for your time,' he said warmly, 'and for pointing out a few problems that I needed to know about.'

Hackman decided that the moment had come to take the plunge.

'Please sit down, my dear fellow,' he said urgently. 'I have a suggestion to make.'

The other man obliged and made

himself comfortable again while the banker swallowed nervously.

'You must understand,' he said, 'that while I am naturally happy to do business with the railroad I also have the good of our little town to consider. Now, supposing the flooding of the creek is a problem that cannot be overcome, and the area to the north would create excavation difficulties, that would seem to leave just one feasible alternative.'

'Such as?'

'Bring the rails through Benson's Butte. Use our water supply, take on cattle and passengers here, and let the railroad claim the credit for reviving the fortunes of the community. The people of the area would be very grateful. Very grateful indeed.'

Mr Sedgwick's eyes narrowed thoughtfully and the banker knew that his stress on the last sentence had not been in vain.

'Grateful, eh,' the surveyor muttered. 'In what way?'

Mr Hackman relaxed. The fish was on the hook.

'Well, you will be put to all the trouble of making a new survey, explaining matters to the Cheyenne office and, of course, you will have more expenses. I feel that on behalf of the town I could suggest that a suitable fee be paid to offset all the outlay.'

'Have you got a suitable fee in mind?'

'I haven't had time to consult the interested parties, but off-hand, I should guess that two thousand dollars would be more than likely.'

Mr Sedgewick smiled frostily. 'My time is big money,' he said tautly, 'so let's forget it, Mr Hackman.'

'I could go as far as three thousand . . . and a half, perhaps . . . '

Mr Sedgewick got to his feet. 'Are you real set on having the rails running through town?' he asked.

'Indeed, yes. I owe it to the people.'

'Well, it's no skin off my nose. I'll want six thousand.'

'That's impossible. This is only a small town.'

'Look, Hackman, I'm taking a risk dealing with you at all. There are ranchers and store owners around here who can raise the cash. Get me two thousand in notes in the next day or two, and the rest when the work starts. That will demonstrate good faith on both sides.'

'You can guarantee the railroad?'

'No, but I can put in the right sort of survey report. I also have enough pull to get away with it. If I do, you owe me another four thousand dollars. If I fail, I'll have at least tried and you'll be out two thousand. Is it a deal?'

He held out his hand and the banker took it eagerly.

10

Mr Sedgewick went down to Macy's corral a very satisfied man. There was a large wad of notes hidden away and he nodded cheerfully to Bill Quince who was saddling his horse and had all the surveying gear ready for loading. Macy stood watching indifferently.

The two men rode off slowly to their work while the smith watched them go with a grin on his face at Sedgewick's control of a horse. He did not hear the marshal approach until the lawman's shadow loomed in front of him.

'You took me by surprise, Marshal,' he said. 'You ain't wearin' spurs.'

'I'm lookin' for Cy,' Matt Sawyer replied. 'Seen him lately?'

'No. Still out of town with the horse he rented. He won't come to no harm, I reckon.'

'Know where he went?'

The man shrugged. 'He was headed towards the Macready spread.'

'Thanks.'

The marshal ambled away to Harry's store and was greeted warmly by the owner who handed him two envelopes he'd been waiting for from Little Bear. He nodded his thanks and went back to the jailhouse to read the contents.

The surveyor and Bill Quince rode steadily on their way towards the north. As they moved, Sedgewick's command of his mount seemed to improve. He rode with more confidence and used only his left hand instead of sawing at the reins amateurishly with both.

'Did you get it?' Bill Quince asked.

'I surely did,' the other man grinned. 'Fifteen hundred dollars in ready money, and the rest to come when the railroad arrives in town. They always fall for it. Better than being in politics.'

He laughed at his own joke but Bill Quince rode glumly at his side.

'You should have taken them for more,' he said angrily.

'I know what I'm doing, for God's sake!' Sedgewick snapped. 'If we stuck out for all the money, they'd watch us like hawks. But just to take them for a little bit and leave them thinking that I'm the fish from the bottom of the pond . . . that's the way to play this game, lad.'

'Fifteen hundred isn't enough. You could have got more.'

'Of course I could, but this is safer. Leave the thinking to me and just play the part you've got. I've left money in my bank account, all my shaving stuff, my bags, and a nearly new pair of boots back there. They've seen us heading out on our usual trail and they're not even curious. By the time they realize they've been taken, we'll be well away.'

'Where do we change horses?'

'We head due west after that wooded rise. There's a ranch that rents remounts for the stage line. According to my map, it's called the S bar B. They'll sell us horses and supplies and return my animal to Macy. You can ditch those measuring poles now, and cover the theodolite with my trail coat. I don't want it damaged. It's too expensive to replace and it's our living.'

He breathed in the sweet smell of the grass. 'We'll stay in Laramie for a while so I can figure out some new pigeons to pluck. This looks like it's going to be a very good year for the Sedgewick, Smith and Sedgewick Company.'

'And I still say we should have taken them for more.'

Sedgewick dismissed the idea impatiently. 'We've made a good living out of this for the last three years. Get too greedy and they hang on to your coat tails; play it cool, and they trust you. Back in that town, they think they're cheating me out of four thousand dollars. That makes them feel good. I'd like to see their faces when they wake up to the truth.'

'I wouldn't. If we were that close, there'd be a lynchin'.'

'There sure as hell would,' Sedgewick laughed. 'What are you figuring to do with your share?'

'Fifteen hundred, you said?'

'Less expenses. That brings it to about twelve hundred. Half of that belongs to you. It's a pile of money for a few weeks' work.'

'What's half of twelve hundred dollars?'

'Six hundred, and it's all yours.'

'Sounds mighty nice, but all them expenses . . . '

'Don't start again. I have to put out money to set everything up. You're getting a good deal and don't forget it. Where the hell would a cowpoke like you pick up six hundred dollars every few weeks?'

'I'm not complainin', it's just that . . . '

'Stow it.'

They rode on in an angry silence.

It was mid-afternoon when they passed through the wide gates of the S bar B spread and headed for the distant ranch house. It was a big building with a wide yard in front of it and a bunkhouse along one side of the yard. Granaries occupied another angle adjacent to newly built stables. The house itself was of stone, limed in a pale yellow and with windows picked out in black.

The two travellers stopped their horses at a respectful distance and waited for permission to alight.

The owner of the ranch came out of the house and surveyed them grimly. Sedgewick raised his hat with old-world politeness.

'Good morning, sir,' he said. 'We are travelling to Benton's Fort and would like to purchase a couple of horses. Our own have travelled a long ways in the past few weeks.'

Sam Benson stepped down from the porch and walked slowly round the two mounts, examining them in detail.

'One of them has been rented in Benson's Butte,' Sedgewick explained. 'If you could have it returned to Macy . . . '

Sam Benson came round to the front again.

'You had business in Benson's Butte?' he asked.

'I was doing a mapping survey there.'

'For the railroad?' Sam Benson's voice brooked no argument.

'Ah, the news has leaked out then.' Sedgewick rose to the occasion. 'You are quite right sir. Our work is finished and we are on our way to the next task.'

'Then I reckon you'd better get down off them animals and take some refreshment.'

'You are too kind.'

'I ain't doin' it for you, but the horses gotta be fed and watered. And we gotta agree a price to make a trade. Your man can go to the cookhouse and you'd better come inside with me.'

He pointed at one of the outbuildings. 'Tell the cook I sent you,' he said to Bill Quince. 'And say a word of thanks to the Almighty before you eat. We're Christian folk here.' He turned and raised his powerful voice. 'Pete, come out here and take care of these horses!'

A door opened in one of the granaries and a cowpoke hurried to obey. He wore a dirty bandage round his throat and, as he got nearer, Bill Quince recognized him.

It was Pete Saker.

11

The injured cowpoke came across to the group of men and reached out for the reins of the horses. Then he raised his head a little and a flash of recognition crossed his face as he saw Bill Quince. He grinned broadly and stepped back a few paces.

'And they say there ain't no justice,' he wheezed. 'I bin waitin' for you, fella, and this time you're wearin' a gun.'

Sedgewick closed his eyes in a gesture of despair while Sam Benson merely stepped out of the line of fire and watched events.

'I ain't lookin' for trouble,' Bill Quince said calmly.

'Well, you sure as hell got some. If you don't draw, I'll blow your head off.'

Pete Saker backed away a few more paces, his hand sliding down to the holster as his body tensed for action.

Quince waited patiently.

'Stop!' The stentorian tones were those of Sam Benson. 'I'll not have any shootin' near the horses. Get them outa the way first.'

Sedgewick took the reins and moved the two mounts to one side. He stood holding the leathers while the two adversaries squared up.

Pete's hand slid down to the butt of the gun with lightning speed and it jerked out of the holster, hammer back and ready to use. A single shot rang out and the horses jumped. There was a smell of burnt powder in the air and some birds flew off a nearby roof.

Saker looked down at his chest. Blood was oozing slowly from his shirt and the Colt was limp in his hand. All eyes went to Bill Quince. He stood with gun raised and recocked in case the dying man pulled the trigger of his own pistol. Pete Saker merely slipped gently to the ground and lay twitching for a few moments.

'Fairly done,' old Sam said with

judicial calm. 'He pulled that gun once too often. I told him time and again but he wouldn't listen. Died bad, too, without the Grace of God. A man always dies bad who don't follow the Way of the Lord.'

'Amen,' murmured Mr Sedgewick thankfully.

A few cowhands had appeared to watch the shoot-out and they carried off the body without any show of regret. Bill Quince had rid them of a bad-tempered bully.

Sedgewick followed the old rancher into the house where large rooms were furnished in a style long out of date. Mrs Benson, a little mouse of a woman, went off to make coffee and fry some bacon for the visitors.

'I believe that your ranch hand and my assistant had some sort of quarrel recently,' Mr Sedgewick ventured.

'So Pete told me. He recognized your man from way back when we took us a herd into Cheyenne. Didn't get his name at the time, but some ranchers across the territory line had been swindled. It seems that a couple of smart dealers took money from them to put a rail line through their local town. Then skedaddled with the cash. Slick operators.'

Sweat was cutting into the dust on Mr Sedgewick's face.

'Yes, of course . . . I only hired Quince in Benson's Butte . . . '

'Untruths are the tools of the Devil.'

'Quite.'

Benson waited while his wife came back with the coffee.

'How much did those people pay you back there?' he asked when the door closed behind her.

'Well . . . I . . . '

'I ain't passin' judgement,' the rancher said bluntly. 'The Almighty will do that in His own good time. He will sort out the good from the bad on the Day of Judgement. What I want to know is, have they caught on to you?'

'No, we rode out this morning, just like normal.'

Benson stood at the window with the coffee cup in his hand. He seemed deep in thought, or prayer. When he turned round to face his visitor, his features had relaxed a little.

'So they'll be expectin' you back tonight?' he asked.

'Yes.'

'You got them maps of yours handy?'

'Yes, they're in my saddle-bag.'

'Go get 'em.'

Sedgewick hurried out and found his way to the corral where the horses had been fed and watered. The saddles and other gear lay against a fence and he hurriedly unpacked his maps and went back to the house. Benson was pouring himself another cup of coffee and there was a distinct smell of brandy in the air. The surveyor spread the main map out on the large veneered table while the rancher leaned over to inspect it.

'So they believe you're goin' to run a railroad through my town,' he mused. 'A right passel of fools they be, and they got what they deserved when they met up with you. Now, I'll tell you something that might save you and your friend from a hangin': I got me some scrub land I want to sell.'

He stared hard at Sedgewick and the surveyor managed a smile.

'My services are at your disposal,' he said gushingly.

'Cut the fancy talk, son. I don't go for townfolk. Now, you listen good, 'cos if you let me down, I swear in the name of the Almighty that I will see you hang.' He pointed a long, bony finger at the map. 'This here strip along Belvale Creek belongs to me. It don't come under the Homestead Act 'cause my pappy claimed it before all that nonsense was thought of. Trouble is, it's been overgrazed and we've had some bad winters so it ain't worth ten cents to the acre. You gettin' my drift?'

'And you want to make a profit out of it?'

'That's right, fella. And not at ten cents an acre. Now if the railroad was buildin' along the creek, they'd pay mighty handsome for it, wouldn't they?'

'They would indeed, Mr Benson.'

'That's what I figured. So it's up to you.'

Sedgewick did some quick calculations and made notes with his silver pencil. 'Well, at a rough guess,' he said carefully, 'they'd need quite a big acreage, right down here and along this line.' He glanced slyly at the rancher. 'Leastways, that's what I'd be telling the folks in town who wanted to buy cheap and sell dear.'

'Not too cheap, fella. Not too cheap.' Old man Benson managed a smile of gratification. 'Well, now, I likes your style, mister,' he said. 'You just get yourself back to town as though you've done another day's work, and start things movin'. Tell that greedy money-lender all casual-like that your survey is done and then show him the new route. Straight through Benson's Butte and across my land on the creek. You can leave the rest to him. He'll be out here to buy my holding as fast as a horse can carry him.'

'There is one more thing, Mr Benson.'

'And what would that be?'

'He'll need to give you a reason to buy useless scrub.'

The rancher scratched his chin. 'I reckon he'll think of somethin',' he said. 'Him bein' on close terms with the Devil and all his works.'

'They'll all be mighty displeased when they find out the truth,' Sedgewick said quietly.

'Won't they just? But you'll be long gone and I don't give a hoot. I'll have turned a profit and that's what it's all about.'

'Tell me, Mr Benson, why didn't you go in with the rest of them when they met and decided to pay me a bribe?'

'Because my pappy didn't raise no donkeys, surveyor man. I'd already spoken to Pete when he got back here with his neck all busted. He couldn't hardly talk none but I got a bit out of him, and I began to wonder what was goin' on in Benson's Butte. So, as soon as Hackman began sayin' his piece, I knew, sure as Hell's a hot place, that you was up to somethin'. So I found me an excuse to go into town. And I'll tell you, fella, that was a hard decision, but I did it and caught a glimpse of the railroad surveyor they was dealin' with. It all fitted with what I'd got from Pete, and when my boys was let outa jail, I had a couple of 'em tail you.'

'Oh, I see.'

'Yessir, they tailed you good, and do you know what they saw?'

'I can guess.'

'Yessir, you didn't do no surveyin'. Just sat around eatin' and smokin'. And that theodolite thing never left its box. I had you dead to rights all set for a hangin'.'

Sedgewick swallowed the rest of his coffee noisily.

'We'd better get started back to town then,' he said nervously. 'It's a long ride.'

'Yeah, and don't get any ideas. My men will be watchin' you from now on. You try headin' for Utah and points west and you'll get almighty dead. You understand me?'

'Yes, Mr Benson.'

Sedgewick and Quince started off for Benson's Butte about an hour later. Their animals had rested and been fed, and the two men were seen off the ranch by Sam Benson himself. He watched until they were out of sight and then turned back to the house, loudly singing 'Rock of Ages' in a rich bass voice.

The surveyor explained the twist that events had taken and his partner listened impatiently until he had finished.

'So we gotta go back there tonight,' he stormed. 'God Almighty! We should have been miles away and safe by then! This might take a few more days and anything can go wrong.'

Sedgewick felt the same way but he was more philosophical.

'It's got to be done,' he said reasonably.

'Going back isn't dangerous. We're part of the scenery now. All I have to do is to have a casual talk with Hackman, tell him that our work is done and show him the new route on the map. He'll take one look and reach for his horse. The truth is that old Benson is a bigger criminal than any of us. And he's doing it legal. I have to admire the rogue. Once we see our banker friend leave town lickity-spit, we're free to go ourselves.'

'We could go now. Head west.'

'Only if you fancy being killed by Benson's men.'

'You could have at least made some money out of this new deal. What the hell are we getting out of it?'

'I'll tell you what we're getting out of it,' Sedgewick snapped. 'We're getting our lives out of it and, believe me, boy, that's the best deal any man can get.'

'I could gun them down. No sweat.'

'One or two of them perhaps, but he must have at least a dozen hands, and he's one vengeful man if ever I saw one.

He told me that God looks over his shoulder.'

They rode a little further and then the surveyor remembered something.

'Try and recall where you dumped those measuring rods. We're going to need them again,' he ordered.

They were late getting into town, and after taking his horse to the corral, the surveyor walked to the hotel and went up to his room. He washed off the trail dust, took a short rest, and then went down to dinner. When he had finished, he strolled through to the saloon for a whiskey at the bar.

He recognized one of Sam Benson's men who was quietly drinking a beer and smiled to himself. He had no intention of playing any double game against the rancher, but it did rile him to do something without turning over a dishonest dollar. He sipped the awful whiskey and promised himself to pick a town with better taste in alcohol for the next job.

The mayor came in for a modest

beer, had a chat with Ma Riley and sidled through a rear door when he thought no one was watching. Nearly an hour passed before the banker came in for a quiet drink. He immediately joined Sedgewick, ordering whiskey for both of them. Ma got the special bottle down and would have joined them if the banker had not given her a slight shake of the head. With a look of annoyance, she retired to the end of the bar to start flirting with Benson's cow hand.

'Had a busy day?' the banker asked.

'Finished this afternoon,' Sedgewick said with tipsy joviality. 'I've done all the field work and now it's just a matter of putting the details down on paper. I'll do that in my room over the next day or so and then be on my way.'

'And the final recommended route?' the banker asked with a touch of anxiety in his voice.

'Slam bang to the outskirts of town, and then off to the north-west. I think you'll be very pleased when you see it on the map.'

'Then it's all set?'

'As well as I can do it. The railroad are getting off pretty lightly anyway. Most of the land we're using is in the public domain and they're only going to have to buy off three or four of the ranchers hereabouts. The few extra miles from the original plan aren't going to matter all that much, so long as the water supply is assured.'

'I can guarantee that,' Hackman said hastily. 'Our supply has never failed.'

'Then it would seem to be settled.'

'You've certainly relieved my mind. Let's have another drink.'

Sedgewick swallowed his whiskey and pulled a face.

'Even Ma's best bourbon is a mite rough on the tongue,' he said. 'Let's go up to my room where I've got a bottle of imported Scotch. The genuine article. And while we're there, I can show you the finalized survey on the map.'

He laid a drunken arm around his companion's shoulder and led the way sedately to the stairs.

After tasting the whiskey in ample measure, the surveyor took a map from the wardrobe and laid it out on his bed. The scar of the proposed route stood out vividly against the printed background. Hackman leaned over it to trace the meandering line avidly. It came to Benson's Butte, then turned north-west along the creek and across the edge of the S bar B ranch. The banker suddenly became sober. His well-honed brain took in the situation at a glance.

'Beautiful,' he said breathlessly. 'A splendid job, my dear friend. I salute you.'

Sedgewick smiled as he poured out more whiskey. He seemed half-asleep.

'These ranchers on the route,' the banker said casually, 'must have been very pleased when you told them that the rails were going over their land.'

'Um?' Mr Sedgewick's look was as blurred as his voice.

'The ranchers. The ones the railroad is buying from.'

'Oh . . . oh, yes. They'll be pleased enough when they're told.'

Sedgewick was resting sleepily against the bedhead now.

'Don't they know about it yet?' the banker probed urgently.

'Not yet.' Sedgewick yawned. 'It's not my job to go around telling them. The company will do that when they get my report.'

His voice tailed off and his head drooped. A bubbly snore was emitted as he slept. Gil Hackman smiled and quietly left the room.

When the door was safely closed, the surveyor opened his eyes and raised himself from the bed. He tucked the map back into its case while he did a little waltz round the room. He'd plucked the same pigeon twice and his self-esteem was repaired. He was a very contented man.

12

Bill Quince was saddling his horse when the marshal came down to Macy's corral. He nodded a greeting to the lawman and began strapping on his saddle-bags and the roll of blankets.

'You're leavin' us then?' the marshal asked.

Quince nodded. 'Mr Sedgewick's offered me a steady job,' he said.

'Well, surveyin' is less risky than bein' a deputy marshal.'

'Yeah, but thanks for the offer. It was right good of you.'

'Oh I thought you might have fitted. Too bad it didn't work out. Good luck, son.'

The marshal wandered back along the street. He was just in time to see Mr Hackman come out of a side lane on his seldom-used gelding. The banker gave the marshal a curt nod and cantered off down the street and out of town.

'That man seems to be in a hell of a hurry,' the lawman said softly to the wooden Indian outside the tobacco store. He went on to the jailhouse and stood at the window, watching whatever was happening on the main street.

The storekeepers were opening their doors. The bank clerk was brushing the dust away from his premises, while a few schoolchildren were walking along noisily to the schoolhouse. Some of them saw him at the window and waved. He grinned and waved back.

Then Mr Sedgewick appeared on the steps of the saloon. The bartender was carrying his luggage and the two men went down to Macy's stable. A gig was waiting there, and the bags were loaded on to it. It was the vehicle that Macy rented out to people who were catching the stage or a train at Chugwater. They would leave it there with the station chief so that he would either hold it until Macy sent out a rider, or could rent it out to someone travelling to Benson's Butte.

Quince mounted his horse and waited for the surveyor to take the reins of the gig. Then the two went out of town together. The bartender walked back to the saloon after putting the tip into his pants pocket.

It was a quiet day in Benson's Butte and Matt Sawyer spent most of it at his two favourite occupations, playing patience or reading his magazine. He never got tired of the West as Ned Buntline saw it.

He had just finished his midday meal when the county sheriff arrived. Matt Sawyer cursed vividly under his breath. The county sheriff was an overbearing, opinionated bully who really got under the hide of everyone with whom he had business. Matt watched him dismount from the tall grey horse and tie it to the hitching rail. He came across the wooden sidewalk with a heavy tread, flinging open the office door with more violence than necessary.

'Howdy, Matt,' he greeted the occupant in a loud voice.

'Mornin', Steve,' the marshal answered quietly. 'Have a cup of coffee?'

'Could certainly use one.'

He took off his over-size stetson, shaking the dust from it all over the floor. His massive frame was lowered into the best chair and he stretched out his booted legs luxuriously.

Matt Sawyer passed over a tin cup of coffee before sitting down again. He scanned the large red face, trying to read something in the piggy eyes that were part-buried in fat. The sheriff was younger than his host, a man in his thirties, tall and heavy, with massive shoulders and pale, bleached hair that was cut short.

He carried a gun on each hip and a Winchester was holstered on his horse. Like most lawmen, he was good with pistol or carbine, and could also break up a bar-room brawl with his fist or boots.

'What brings you to Benson's Butte? the marshal asked.

'You do, Matt. You sent a message to Tolly Lincoln at Little Bear askin' for any information he might have on a Bill Quince or anyone answerin' that description. You also sent another message to Cheyenne by telegraph. You were quick off the mark, Matt. The marshal at Cheyenne sends his compliments.'

'That's kind of him,' Matt responded dryly. 'So you're after this Bill Quince?'

'Sure as hell. Quince probably ain't his real name. He was Doug Crawford a year or so back in Denton's Fort when he shot a man.'

'Murder?'

'Maybe, maybe not; but he lit out so we have to track him down. I didn't reckon on catchin' up with him until you started askin' questions. Soon as I could, I took me off to Benson's Butte. Where is he?'

'You've missed him by quite a few hours. He left town early this mornin' with his new boss. They're probably headin' for Chugwater.'

'I'll get me after them then.'

Sheriff Robarts rose from his chair and hitched up his guns.

'Why were you enquirin' after him, Matt?' he asked.

'Oh, I thought he might make a deputy marshal.'

Robarts grinned ferociously. 'Well, he can use a gun,' he conceded. 'I'll bring him back to your jailhouse when I catch up with him. I've got another call to make so it might be a week or two before I can take him to Cheyenne. Mike Stanker's sons are feudin' again over at Still Creek so I gotta knock their fool heads together or they'll shoot up the whole area.'

The sheriff stamped out of the office to mount his long-suffering horse. The marshal stood in the doorway watching him going down the main street at a brisk canter. A gig was entering town at a spanking pace and the sheriff drew alongside of it to exchange words with the driver.

Matt Sawyer strained his eyes to see what was happening and then fetched the large, brass-bound telescope to make things better. Bill Quince was driving the gig, his own horse tied to the rear of the vehicle. There was no sign of Sedgewick. The sheriff was now escorting the gig to the office of the town doctor. The marshal put on his hat and hurried out to see what was going on.

When he got there, the sheriff was helping an injured Bill Quince off the rig and up the sidewak to the doctor's door. A bloody bandanna was wrapped tightly about the upper part of the cowpoke's left leg while semi-congealed blood cut a bright swathe down his pants to below the knee. His face was drawn in pain and the marshal followed into the surgery. The doctor was at home and helped to lay the man on a couch.

'Slug's still in there,' he said. 'I'll give you some chloroform, son, so you'll just pass out and not feel a thing. Don't worry, now, it ain't hit nothin' important and you'll be as good as new in a couple of weeks or so. Now, just lie back and breathe natural like.'

He held the gauze mask over Bill Quince's face and dealt out the drops of anaesthetic from the little brown bottle.

'Did he tell you what happened, Steve?' Matt Sawyer asked the sheriff.

'Yeah. It seems him and his boss was bush-whacked on the trail. The other guy was killed and this one was hit in the leg. He didn't get off a single shot, it was all over so fast.'

'Did he recognize anyone?'

'He reckons not. Just two or three men came at them from behind a clump of rocks.'

'And where's Sedgewick now?'

'That the other fella?'

'Yes, he was drivin' the gig.'

'He's outside in it now. Let's go take a look.'

The two men hurried out into the

clean sunlight, pushing their way through the crowd that had gathered. Cyrus B. Sedgewick of Sedgewick, Smith and Sedgewick, lay on his back with his knees doubled beneath him to fit the available space. A single bullet had gone through the centre of his chest, probably penetrating his heart. The sheriff leaned into the gig to go through the dead man's pockets. There was a penknife, some coins, half-a-dozen bullets, and a small silver pencil.

'No big money,' he said discontentedly.

'And no gold watch and chain,' the marshal added. 'Did Quince mention them bein' robbed?'

'Yeah. After they was shot, the bushwhackers grabbed this fella's watch, his wallet, and then high-tailed it. He looks like a city dude. They can always be reckoned to carry plenty of cash money.'

'Yes, has he got a gun?'

'No, he must have been relyin' on our wounded cowpoke. And that *hombre* is sure goin' to be surprised when he wakes up and finds he's wanted for a killin' at Denton's Fort.'

The marshal gazed around at the assembled crowd and was just about to send them on their way when he spotted the banker hovering in the background. He pushed his way through to him.

'Afternoon, Mr Hackman. I take it you know who's dead back there?'

'Yes, a customer came in to tell us that Mr Sedgewick had been murdered. Is it true then?'

'Dead as a pole-axed steer. Would you like to see the body?'

'No ... no ... thank you,' the banker hesitated. 'We, that is, some of the business community entrusted Mr Sedgewick with a sum of money ...'

The marshal looked interested. 'Did you now? Why should that be?'

'Well, you know how banking is. Some cash had to be sent to Chugwater, and since Sedgewick was travelling in that direction, we thought he might carry it for us.'

152

'You're very trusting, Mr Hackman. After all, you've only known him for a little over a week.'

'Oh he's well vouched for,' the banker replied hastily. 'But . . . the money . . . is it safe?'

'I'm afraid not. He was robbed.'

'Oh, dear!' The banker was genuinely upset. He had hoped to recover the cash that he had paid out and hated to see good money go to waste.

'How much money would it be?' the marshal asked.

Gil Hackman felt it best to tell the truth on that point in case the robbers were ever caught.

'Two thousand dollars,' he said in a small voice. 'In ten-dollar bills.'

The marshal whistled. 'That's a heap of cash,' he murmured, 'and a mighty awkward handful. Why didn't you give him bigger notes?'

'Ten-dollar bills are the largest we normally use in Benson's Butte. Most people get nervous if they see anything larger.'

'Yeah, I don't rightly recollect seein' anythin' bigger myself. Well, you can kiss your money goodbye, Mr Hackman. Somebody will be a'spendin' of it in another state by this time next week.'

The banker nodded sad agreement. 'What about his equipment?' he asked with sudden urgency.

'Still in the gig,' the marshal told him. 'Somethin' worryin' you, Mr Hackman?'

'No, certainly not. It's just that all his plans for the railroad are in those bags. The work would be wasted if they were stolen.'

'They're safe enough and we'll get them to the railroad people,' the marshal said dryly.

He went back to where the sheriff was supervising the removal of the body. The man from the funeral parlour was there, giving matters his professional attention while he tried to find out who was going to pay for the funeral.

'It's too late in the day to form a posse and set out after that bunch,' Steve Robarts said when they arrived back at the jailhouse. 'I reckon to gettin' me a night's sleep and settin' off in the mornin'. Got any names in mind for this sort of thing, Matt?'

The marshal shook his head. 'We've not had anything like this for the best part of two years. The Purvis boys was hung and that seemed to quiet things down in the county.'

Sheriff Robarts smiled contentedly. 'Yeah, I reckon they was glad to be hung after the rough time I gave 'em,' he chuckled. 'Billy Purvis thought he was tough but I sure as hell cut the bastard down to size.'

'You did that, Steve,' the marshal agreed bleakly. 'They got more than two thousand dollars off Sedgewick,' he went on, as he poured out the coffee.

'That's big money. Is there a reward?'

'Well, the local banker says it belongs

155

to him, but he never mentioned no reward. Odd, come to think of it. Banks carry some sort of insurance these days.'

'Maybe he was too fussed at the time. Bankers get right upset when they lose money.'

'Ain't that the truth,' the marshal muttered.

He told Sheriff Robarts of his conversation with Gil Hackman and also mentioned some of his suspicions. The sheriff listened in silence, his heavy face fixed in concentration.

'So you reckon that some of your worthy citizens have been greasin' the palm of the railroad surveyor to bring the tracks through here?' he asked after a while.

'I think it's likely,' the marshal said. 'It would explain the closeness of Hackman and Sedgewick and it could also explain why Hackman has been ridin' out of town. He's not a man who likes travellin' rough so there has to be a reason for his visitin' folks. There's another point, too: if they were bushwhacked for the money, then it has to be by somebody who knew what was happening. There are no outsiders involved.'

13

Sheriff Robarts took his formidable bulk around the town, asking questions, staring hard at folk, and generally intimidating everyone he came across. The marshal let him carry on with it. He felt a little too old for wandering about in the heat, and he knew the people involved and had to live with them until he could manage to retire. He sat outside the jailhouse with his feet on the hitching rail watching his colleague cross and recross the street as he interrogated his way around Benson's Butte.

The sheriff decided to stay the night. He had gathered enough information to feel that he was on to something and he also wanted to question Bill Quince some more when he recovered from the chloroform. The marshal let Robarts sleep in one of the cells and, bright and early the next morning, the visiting lawman was out again, his guns snugly on his hips and his great bulk looming over the town.

He returned for a midday meal in a satisfied mood.

'The way I see it, Matt,' he said between mouthfuls of food, 'is that one or more of the ranchers was in on the bribery, and one of them sent his men after the surveyor. I've taken that banker fella to pieces and he's one sweatin' man. He practically admits that he and the cattle owners was bribin' the Sedgewick fella and that the money he was carryin' was what they'd paid him. So, I reckon it has to be one of five people behind the bush-whackin'.'

The marshal had finished eating and was lighting a cigar.

'And who would they be?' he asked with studied innocence.

'Well, there's the banker for a start, but he'd have to hire some outside help to do it. The likeliest are Jacob

Macready, whose spread Hackman admits they used for the plannin' of the bribery: then there's George Martin, Sam Benson, and Doug Winfield.'

The marshal smiled. 'Our local money man really spilled the beans to you, Steve,' he said with feigned admiration.

'I don't play nursery games. I lean heavy.'

'I'll bet you do just that. Maybe I can be of help on this matter. Sam Benson didn't join the others and, from what I gather he sent some of his boys into town to shoot the place up. He wanted to make us look bad so that the railroad wouldn't build through here. However, he did know about the bribe; he has some mighty tough boys, and he's a Holy Joe who can justify anything because God is on his side. To cap it all, one of his men has been tailin' Sedgewick and followed him and Quince out of town this mornin'.'

'Is that a fact now? You don't miss much.'

'I see a lot from this window.'

'Well, that seems to clinch it. I've heard of Benson and how his family started this town, but I've never actually met him.'

'You should. It could be an interestin' meetin'. He has a lot to gain by us not gettin' the railroad and he makes no secret of his hatred for Benson's Butte. All the same, bushwhackin' don't seem his way of handlin' things.'

'Maybe I'll ride out to his place after I've had a talk with Doug Crawford, or Quince, or whatever he's callin' himself these days.'

'The doc tells me he's a little better this mornin'. If he can give you a description of the men who attacked him, you might find them at the S bar B, but I have my doubts.'

'I think I will find them there. I gotta hunch, Matt.'

The sheriff pulled out his large silver watch.

'I'll go have a word with this Quince fella now, and then I may take me off to

Benson's ranch. Unless I'm told something different, that is. You'll keep Quince here in case I'm away a few days?'

'Sure. I'll jail him just as soon as he's fit to walk.'

The sheriff rode off and his horse was hitched outside the doctor's office for over an hour. The marshal sat idly on the porch again, watching everything with a detached air and was not surprised to see the sheriff finally remount and head out of town. He smiled gently, tapped out his pipe and strolled casually towards the doctor's house.

Doc Merton was out on a visit and an elderly housekeeper, who also acted as nurse and midwife, admitted Matt Sawyer and led him to the little bedroom where Bill Quince lay propped up in a narrow cot.

'How you feelin', Bill?' the marshal asked, as he took a chair.

'Could be worse,' the man answered cheerfully. 'The doc says I'll be able to walk in a few days.'

'Good. Then you can come and stay with me at the jailhouse.'

'You arrestin' me, Marshal?' There was no surprise in the man's voice.

'Not on my own account, but Sheriff Robarts has a warrant for you on a murder charge. I'm holdin' you till he gets back. That's the law, son.'

'It wasn't murder Marshal. I shot him in self-defence.'

'I ain't arguin' the toss, Bill. I'm just doin' what the law tells me to do. You'll get a jury trial in Cheyenne.'

'And a neck-tie party.'

'Every time you pull a gun, that's the risk you take.'

'I meant to ask the doc and I forgot: are my bags and blankets safe?'

'They're safe enough. Macy's lookin' after them.'

'Thanks. And Mr Sedgewick's stuff?'

'That's in my office. We'll auction it off to pay for the burial unless some relative turns up.'

'When's he bein' buried?'

'Tomorrow, I guess.'

'I would have liked to be there. He was a decent boss.'

'Yeah. Now tell me, son, exactly what happened out there on the trail? Take your time. We got all day.'

'Well, I told the sheriff . . . '

'Don't fret about him. He's gone off to Sam Benson's place to see what the Almighty looks like at close quarters.'

'He's wastin' his time. I didn't recognize the men who attacked me. I told him that.'

'All right, so start at the beginning.'

Bill Quince shifted on the bed to get more comfortable. The room was heating up under the warm sun and even the open window could not cool it off to any degree. The white net curtains hung limply, only disturbed by an occasional blowfly as it brushed against them with a loud humming noise.

'We got as far as that long dip where there's a clump of rocks on either side of the trail, about six or seven miles out of town. We was ridin' slow and talkin' some, and I figure neither of us was paying much attention. Two fellas suddenly rode out from behind the rockpile on the left and waved guns. I pulled on them, but never got off a bullet. I heard three or four shots let loose and one of them caught me in the leg. My horse spooked and threw me, so I just lay there, tryin' to stop the blood. There was a lotta ruckus all round 'cause the riders were back and forth and their horses was kickin' up one hell of a dust. I heard one or two more shots, and I think there might have been a third rider, but I couldn't swear to that. Then it was all over. They rode off and Mr Sedgewick was dead.'

Sawyer took out his pipe before changing his mind and lighting a stogie instead.

'Which way did they ride?' he asked.

'I don't know. I was still bleedin' bad and tryin' to tie a neckerchief round my leg. When I finally got up, Mr Sedgewick was lying on the ground and the rig had moved off quite a ways. My horse had followed it. I collected the animals, brought them back, and heaved him into the rig. Then I just lit back to town for help.'

'And you didn't recognize anyone?'

Bill Quince shook his head. 'No, they was just cowpokes. One was tall and wore one of them big stetsons. Light colour it was. The other was all belly. I'd certainly never laid eyes on him before. He had a Mexican saddle.'

The marshal raised his eyebrows. 'Mexican? Did you tell the sheriff that?' he asked, with a trace of amusement in his voice.

'I reckon so, why?'

'Sam Benson uses a Mexican saddle.'

'It weren't Sam Benson.'

'How do you know?'

'I saw him in town when he came to get his men outa jail.'

The answer was quick but the marshal detected something wrong with it.

'You and Sedgewick didn't visit the S

bar B by any chance?' he asked sharply.

'No . . .'

'Don't lie to me, son. I'll soon find out.'

'Well, yeah, we did go there.'

'Why?'

'I don't rightly know. Sedgewick said he had some business with Sam Benson and he was in the house for about an hour.'

Matt Sawyer thought things over for a few minutes in silence.

'Pete Saker is one of Benson's men,' he said. 'Did you see him out there?'

Quince moved uneasily in the bed.

'Marshal . . .'

'Don't play dummy, son. The sheriff will bring back the truth.'

'All right, so Pete Saker was there. He drew on me and I killed him. It was fair and square and there were plenty of witnesses. Mr Benson himself put the blame on Pete.'

'Well, don't worry about that killin'; nobody's goin' to charge you with the death of Pete Saker. He was a bad lot.

I've often wondered though how he recognized you from some other place. Any ideas?'

The other man shook his head. Then he suddenly grinned, almost as though he was relieved.

'I guess he knew I was a wanted man. Maybe I got my picture on a bill.'

'You're not that important, son. Did Sedgewick have any money on him?'

'I guess so. He paid my wages and stayed in the best room at Ma Riley's.'

'I mean big money. Real big money.'

'I don't know. I reckon he wouldn't tell the hired help. He had a pretty large pigskin wallet that was well stuffed with notes, but nothin' more than that.'

'Was there any sign of a search when you reached his body?'

'Oh, sure. His pockets had been ransacked and his watch and chain was missin'. They hadn't touched his luggage, though!'

The marshal stood up. 'Well, get yourself better. I'll come again in the next few days.'

He waved a cheery farewell and left the room.

Out in the open air again, the marshal took a deep breath to clear his lungs of the medicine-like atmosphere of the doctor's house. He walked slowly down to Macy's smithy to make sure that Quince's saddle and other belongings were being well looked after. Macy was working at the forge and waved the lawman to the barn where they were stored.

Matt Sawyer left after about ten minutes and went back to the jailhouse to await events. He sat at his desk and stared at the luggage of the dead surveyor. He had searched it thoroughly, noting every little item in his ledger, but it told him nothing. The theodolite lay on his desk in its mahogany case. He opened it up and took out the instrument. It meant nothing to him. A complete mystery. The ivory scales of figures and the eyeglass were a puzzle. He peered through the lens and twiddled the knobs. A piece of paper lay in the bottom of the case and he pulled it out curiously. It was an explanatory leaflet. The marshal read it carefully, but was still not enlightened, and turned the wooden case round in his hands. It was heavy and solid, marked by a great deal of travel. The lining was torn slightly here and there.

He picked up the theodolite and wrapped it once more in its white cloth. Then he turned the case round to repack the instrument. There was a very slight rattling noise from the wooden box. He shook it vigorously; something was hidden behind the lining.

14

The town cooled off as the sun vanished below the horizon and a brisk wind blew up as it often did. The marshal had finished his evening meal and had smoked a leisurely cigar before walking down to Ma's place to see who was gathered there. The saloon was still being repaired, but the bulk of the work had been done and the only real difference was that the gilt mirror had not been replaced.

Ma was behind the bar, talking to the banker and the mayor. The marshal bought himself a beer before going over to join them.

'All you folks have been talkin' to the sheriff, I hear,' he greeted them cheerfully.

Ma Riley looked slightly embarrassed while the banker stared at the lawman uneasily. The mayor looked from one to the other and hastily finished his drink.

'I'd better be getting on home,' he said. 'My dear wife . . . '

'Stay for a while, Mr Mayor,' the marshal said firmly. 'This is official business. Not just a friendly chat.'

He put down his glass on the bar and confronted the three of them.

'Let me tell you what I've seen happening in the last week or so,' he said quietly. 'I've seen two strangers come to town who suddenly team up and do some surveyin'. At first, we're told it's a map-makin' job, and then the news leaks out that they're workin' for the railroad. That causes a real heap of interest among our prominent citizens. Mr Hackman here goes ridin' outa town. He starts frequentin' Ma's place and havin' meetings with the mayor. Then the two strangers finish their work and ride off — with a heap of money, accordin' to Mr Hackman. Money that's bein' carried on behalf of the bank. Then, when the sheriff asked questions in a rougher sort of way than

I'd use, we hear that Mr Hackman actually gave the money to the surveyor. It didn't belong to the bank at all. Now, the sheriff doesn't have my trustin' nature, so he jumped to the idea that somebody bribed the surveyor to put the rails through Benson's Butte.'

'It was not a bribe,' the banker asserted in a quavering tone. 'The man did some extra surveying on behalf of local ranchers and he was paid an additional fee. The final route was his own affair.'

'Mr Hackman, I don't give the twitch of a cow's ass about the bribe,' Matt Sawyer said bluntly. 'If you get the railroad through this town, I'd person-ally put up a monument to you. But there ain't no railroad. You've been took.'

There was a long silence, and then the banker began to laugh.

'Now, Marshal,' he chuckled, 'you don't know the whole story. Not only do we get the railroad to come through town, but old Sam Benson has sold me some land of his that the tracks have to pass through. You just don't know what's going on in this town.'

'Matt Sawyer, you're gettin' old,' Ma Riley said cruelly. 'Why don't you put up your guns and screw your butt into a rockin' chair?'

The marshal did not get ruffled. 'I'm certainly thinkin' of doin' just that,' he said. 'In fact, since the mayor is here, I can hand in my badge right now. Or if that will discommode the town, I'll serve out a month's notice.'

'Now, Marshal,' the mayor intervened hastily, 'let's not take offence. Ma didn't really mean what she said. The town has done very well with you as law officer.'

'No, I've said my piece and I'm goin' to retire. You see, when I tell you what has happened here — and what is goin' to happen — I reckon you'll want a new marshal anyway.'

'I think you'd better explain yourself, Sawyer,' the banker said pompously. 'I have just managed a deal that will put this little town on the map and I'm not having some broken-down old gun-slinger telling me that I've been made a fool in the process.'

'Well, you have, and if you'll hold your gab, I'll tell you how.'

'We'll listen, Matt,' the mayor said in a conciliatory tone.

'All right. So you did your deal with Sedgewick. How much cash money did you actually give him?'

'Two thousand dollars in tens,' said the banker. 'Exactly as I told you on the street.'

'That figures. And now I'll tell you what you didn't tell me. You promised him more, but he didn't grab at it. Just said he'd collect the rest when the rails went through. I figure that suited you down to the ground because you were goin' to tell him to eat a cow-pat if he turned up for the rest of the money. After all, what could he do? He couldn't go runnin' to the sheriff or the marshal, could he?'

The mayor decided to be on the side

of the angels. He moved a little further away from Gil Hackman and assumed an official air.

'Perhaps you'd better explain, Marshal,' he said grimly.

'It's quite easy, really. Sedgewick and his sidekick, Quince, are a couple of flim-flam men. They travel from town to town doin' map surveyin' and leavin' enough little clues about for people to think that they're workin' for the railroad. Then some smart operator offers them money to change the route, nearer to the town, or nearer to his ranch. Oh, they're good. Maps prepared and left in hotel rooms; visitin' cards from railroad officials . . . '

He looked at Ma Riley who blushed furiously.

'They're smart as paint,' he went on. 'The pigeon they're pluckin' does all the work and, when he's hooked, they don't get greedy. Just two or three thousand dollars at a time. Then they ride on to pull the trick somewhere else. They took you, Hackman. They saw you for a nice fat pigeon and they plucked you good.'

The banker tried to bluster. His face was pale but he managed a confident smile.

'I don't believe any of this,' he said bravely. 'I searched the room ... I found everything out for myself. He had to admit that ... '

His voice trailed off as the marshal nodded happy agreement.

'That's the way he worked; Quince is the gunslinger in case things go wrong. He comes into town as a trail bum and they meet up because some fool marshal like me introduces them. Oh, they were a tricky pair, gentlemen. The best I've seen.'

'How did you find out about all this, Marshal?' the mayor asked calmly.

'Oh, just a bit at a time,' Matt Sawyer said. 'When I first came across Quince, I reckoned he was no ordinary cowpoke. He was too good even without a gun. So I suggested a deputy's job. I sent off a few messages to Little Bear.

Gave his description to other lawmen. One of the answers that came back was that he and a dandified city fella were swindlin' honest bankers and ranchers. I knew I had him dead to rights then. The pair of them also made a mistake. Quince apparently came to town without a gun. All part of his trailbum act. Sedgewick told me that he'd buy him one. But he didn't. There's only one store in town sellin' guns and they didn't do business with either Quince or Sedgewick. So he had a gun in his saddle-bag all the time.'

'Did you know he was wanted for murder on a county warrant?' the mayor asked.

'Yep. That was one of the messages I got back from Little Bear.'

'Then why the hell didn't you arrest him?' the banker shouted.

'I'm a town marshal and I did my job when I let the county authorities know he was here. That's why the sheriff came to town.'

'You could have warned us,' the

mayor said reproachfully.

'I reckon so, but you see, Mayor, if I'd said anythin' at all, Mr Hackman here would have denied that he was payin' bribes and all his rancher friends would have been horrified at me sullyin' their good names. So I figured I ought to watch how things developed.'

There was a long, uncomfortable silence. Hackman looked distinctly ill; Ma Riley was on the verge of tears, and only the mayor remained cool.

'I see your point, Marshal,' he said with the precision of a legal mind, 'but you have him now. He's at Doc Merton's place.'

The marshal looked at the banker. 'I think, Mr Mayor,' he said quietly, 'that arrestin' this fella on a fraud charge would be very embarrassin' for a lot of prominent folk. Much better to let the sheriff take him to Cheyenne for the murder. With the sort of justice they got there he'll likely hang. Then it could all be forgot. No gossip, no public scandal . . . '

The mayor nodded eager agreement. His agile mind had been working along the same lines.

'I think that would be the best way, Marshal,' he said. 'You agree, Hackman?'

The unfriendly tone hit the money-lender like a bullet.

'But the money . . . ' he began.

'Damn the money!' the mayor bawled. 'More fool you for giving it to him.'

'You can kiss the money goodbye,' the marshal said bleakly. 'It's long gone.'

15

It had turned midnight when the sheriff rode into town and unsaddled his horse at Macy's corral. He trudged wearily to the jailhouse where he found the marshal waiting for him. The air of the office was thick with tobacco smoke and the lingering aroma of strong coffee. The sheriff thankfully helped himself to a mug of it.

'I got the bastards,' he said, as he sat down heavily. 'Got 'em dead to rights. That Sam Benson and two of his men: the fella with the big gut that Quince mentioned and another guy whose gun was still dirty. He'd fired three shots and not cleaned it.'

'Where are they now?' Matt Sawyer asked mildly.

The big man flushed. 'That Sam Benson's got hisself fourteen or fifteen hands and they all tote guns. I had to back down and I don't take kindly to that. I'm collectin' me a posse and goin' back there. I'll bring them in if I have to shoot up the whole place.'

'I don't think Benson is responsible.'

'Well, I'm tellin' you that I've got them sure as shootin'. Benson even rides a horse with a Mexican saddle. Just like the young fella said.'

The marshal got up to pour himelf more coffee.

'Steve,' he said quietly, 'if you mix it with Sam Benson, you'll have one hell of a fight on your hands. He's tough and his pride is somethin' to make Lucifer blush. Mix it with him and there'll be blood all over the county. I don't think his men did this and I'm playin' no part in it. You get your own posse together, but I won't be askin' any of the townfolk to join it. They got more sense.'

'What about you? Are you goin' to sit on your ass?'

'Yes. I quit marshaling earlier tonight and I retire at the end of the month. If you want to put it legal-like, the S bar B is outside my jurisdiction: I'm town marshal. But I'm tellin' you, Steve, I know all the local folk, and Sam Benson didn't bushwhack nobody.'

'So that's your opinion. I got mine and I'm ridin' out to arrest them tomorrow.'

'Look, Steve, didn't you ask the cowpoke with the dirty gun why it was in that state?'

'Sure I did, but he said what they all say when they're caught. He was shootin' at varmints and hadn't time to clean it.'

'He may have been tellin' the truth.'

'He looked as guilty as hell.'

'Your way of treatin' folk makes them all feel guilty. They take one look at your face and confess to shootin' Abe Lincoln.'

'I'm goin' to bed,' the sheriff growled. 'I got respect for you, Matt, but you've been in this town a long time and you're too friendly with the locals. Now, me, I keeps my distance.

That way I can see things clear.'

Matt Sawyer grinned. 'You're possibly right, Steve, but I'm too old a hound to learn new tricks. Maybe it's as well I'm retirin'.'

The sheriff wasted two hours the next morning trying to inspire the local men with an urge to accompany him to the Benson spread. He got no takers and rode angrily out of town to see if he could pick up a posse in Little Bear. Everybody watched him go with a certain malicious pleasure.

The marshal mounted up soon afterwards and set out at a slow pace in the increasing heat. He smoked as he rode, giving the horse its head and gently musing on what he would be doing at the end of the month. He had vague plans, but his main thought was to get rid of the marshal's badge and live like an ordinary citizen.

He reached the draw where the trail dipped into what had once been a stream and where rocks were piled up on either side. A few tufts of bunch grass grew raggedly at the base of the rocks and a couple of small birds sat watching him from the top of a dead tree trunk. He dismounted and tethered his horse to the tree, much to the annoyance of the birds who flew off screeching their rage.

Matt Sawyer took off his hat to wipe the sweaty brow beneath it. He moved slowly round the rocks, examining the ground and looking at every snake and lizard track with all the expertise of a life spent in the area. He came back to the trail and walked carefully through the draw, his head bent and his eyes alert for every sign of an attack by two or three men on a gig and a single horseman. The marshal worked patiently, with the tenacity of experience, and when he had what he wanted, he mounted his horse and rode back to town.

His first call was to the doctor's house. He didn't go to see the patient, but headed straight for the medical man's office.

'Doc,' he said urgently, 'have you still got the bullet you took out of Bill Quince?'

'Sure. I thought you might be asking. I've also got the one out of Sedgewick. It lodged in his back.'

He opened a little drawer in the big roll-top desk and produced the two bullets. The marshal looked at them carefully.

'Which one is out of Quince's leg?' he asked.

'The slightly smaller one. The other's the usual .45. It's a bit damaged by hitting bone but quite easy to recognize. Why the interest?'

'It always helps to know what sort of gun was used,' the marshal said vaguely. He looked at the smaller bullet. 'This seems to be a .41. Were either of them fired at close range?'

The doctor shrugged. 'There was some scorching on Quince's pants if that's what you mean. But don't ask me the range. I'm a doctor of medicine, not a Pinkerton man.'

'Thanks, Doc. If you'd ever like to join the forces of law and order, I can mention your name to the mayor as my replacement.'

The doctor said something unprintable as the grinning marshal left the office.

It was a couple of hours later that Sheriff Robarts arrived back in town. He was looking flustered and had all the appearance of a man who had travelled hard. His horse was lathered and stood with its head low at the hitching rail. The marshal watched his colleague slake his thirst at the water jug and then went out to unsaddle the tired horse while the sheriff brushed himself down.

'You look like you rode hard, Steve,' he said, trying not to grin at the man's obvious discomfort.

'Matt, I got me a whole heap of trouble,' the sheriff confessed. 'Old man Benson is on my tail and he's threatenin' a lynchin'.'

'Is he now? Well, if he's threatenin' I

reckon he's in a mood to do it.'

'Matt, you gotta quiet the old bastard down. He's gone insane.'

'Very likely. I always did think he was weaned on loco weed. Where's your posse?'

It was a cruel question and intended to be.

'I got no posse, Matt. They all lit out on me.'

'You'd better tell me about it before Benson turns up with the necktie party.'

'I rode to Little Bear and picked eleven men who were willin' to ride for a posse fee. We went out to Benson's ranch and I faced him down about the saddle, the cowpoke with the dirty gun and the other one with the big belly. I told him that they were under arrest.'

Matt Sawyer whistled. 'You sure do make waves, Steve. What happened then?'

'Benson practically foamed at the mouth. Said I was a spawn of Satan and hell-bent on persecutin' the righteous. You should have heard him, Matt. He was pure loco. Then the guy with the gut took a swing at me with his fist, so I drew. Well . . . all hell broke loose. Everybody dived for cover and two of my men got shot up. I think one of Benson's men was hit and someone opened a corral to turn out a passel of steers. We was swamped, Matt. The steers just swept us away like water. All my men went off fit to be frightened jack-rabbits; I reckon they're still ridin'.'

The marshal tried to keep a straight face. 'I wouldn't be surprised,' he said. 'So you left without your prisoners?'

'The odds bein' what they were, I high-tailed it as fast as I could. Benson was standin' in the middle of the yard shoutin' for his horse and screamin' that he'd see me hanged for murder if his man died.'

He stopped talking and huddled in the chair. 'They can't do that, can they?'

'Times is changin', Steve. If you went in there and started a gun fight, you're in trouble. I told you that Benson and his men had nothing to do with this. If the real killer is nabbed, you're in it deep; and if you slew one of his men, then it's murder And I don't think bein' the county sheriff will save you.'

'But I had them dead to rights. They're guilty.'

'No, Steve. Now, you'd better listen to me and listen well. Sam Benson doesn't bluff. He's goin' to ride into Benson's Butte and he'll have a posse of his own to back him. The other ranchers might ride with them and that means that we could have forty or fifty armed men after your hide. Now, I'm the only lawman in town and I can't hold them off. What happened at the S bar B is not my business, but what happens in this town is. If one of Benson's men is dead and you're accused of murder, I'll have to make an arrest and hand you over to the county sheriff.'

'But I am the county sheriff!'

'There'll be a new one the minute

Cheyenne knows what's happened. You're in real trouble.'

'My God! I was just tryin' to do my job!'

'Of course, if you weren't in town, I couldn't arrest you,' the marshal said softly.

'My horse can't go no further tonight. If I could borrow . . .'

'Not mine, Steve. That would be too suspicious. If I were in your boots, I'd go down to Macy's, get one of his hire horses and leave your animal there to rest up. Then I'd be out of town as if the whole Apache nation was at my heels.'

The sheriff got to his feet with pathetic eagerness. 'I'll do that, Matt. Thanks; you're a friend.' He turned as he reached the door. 'And you'll hold on to Quince for me?'

'Of course I will.'

Matt Sawyer sat back in his chair and enjoyed a good long laugh once the sheriff was safely out of the way. He had no doubt that Sam Benson would come

191

riding into town, but he also knew that the old rancher was not going to lynch anybody or disturb the peace when he could use the courts to squeeze money out of a law-breaking lawman. The marshal started making more coffee in case the rancher was thirsty when he arrived.

Sam Benson turned up in the early hours of the morning. He was accompanied by two of his men, one of whom went straight to the doctor's surgery while the other stabled the horses and arranged lodging at Ma Riley's for his boss. The men would be left to sleep with the mounts. The rancher entered the jailhouse and sat himself down without preamble. He took the offered cup of coffee and gulped thankfully.

'Is he here?' he asked in his deep voice.

'No, he lit out as soon as he could change horses,' the marshal said cheerfully. 'Seemed to be scared that some ragin' madman was comin' to lynch him. I didn't bother to tell him different.'

'I'd as soon lynch him as spit,' the rancher growled, 'but the Almighty tells us to forgive our enemies.'

'So He does, and you can also take him to court in Cheyenne for attackin' you and your people. Could be a profitable little shoot-up, Sam — if you didn't bushwhack Sedgewick and Quince.'

The rancher looked hard at the marshal under his bushy brows.

'You know me better than that, Matt Sawyer,' he said. 'That surveyor fella was as crooked as Satan's tail. He and his sidewinder of a partner swindled all the smart folk around here, but they didn't hogwash me. Pete saw to that. So I used 'em, Matt.'

The marshal grinned and poured more coffee. 'So I hear. And you got rid of some land at the right price. Sam Benson, you're a shrewd old goat, and I reckon the Devil speaks to you even more than the Almighty. You play both sides of the fence.'

'Don't take the name of the Lord in vain. He is always on the side of the righteous.'

'Then how come He's on talkin' terms with you?'

The rancher refused to be insulted and hugged the coffee mug between his hands.

'You must have a reason for bein' in town again,' the marshal hinted.

'Sure have. I was hopin' the sheriff was still here. If he had been, I'd have laid an official complaint against him for shootin' up my home and woundin' one of my hired help. He's gotta pay damages for that. Big damages.'

'I can't argue the point, but he's on his way back to Cheyenne and it's there you'll have to travel. I moved him on because I didn't want Benson's Butte mixed up in it. I like a quiet life here. You know, Sam, I reckon you cottoned on to Sedgewick long before I did. Why in hell's name didn't you tell me?'

The rancher narrowed his eyes

cannily. 'I look to my own affairs first,' he said.

'Yeah, so I see. Well, you must be laughin' up your sleeve to see Hackman an' the other ranchers down on the deal by a few thousand dollars.'

'I don't laugh at the misfortunes of others, Matt Sawyer, even when they cheat and go against the teachin' of the Good Book. But there is joy in my heart when the unGodly are brought to justice.'

'Well, if you'd been here when the sheriff arrived, there'd have been joy in your wizened old heart and no mistake.'

The marshal told him of the lawman's panic and the rancher's shoulders began to heave as he took in the story. A grating noise came from his lips that could have been interpreted as laughter. There were even little tears in the corner of each eye.

'Well, it was worth a long ride just to hear that story,' he said as he rose from his seat. 'And now I shall go to that den of evil that Ma Riley calls a hotel, where

I shall sleep the sleep of the just.'

'I'm sure you will, Sam, and if you can't nod off, she has a new girl by the name of Millie . . .'

The old rancher fled from the jailhouse and Matt Sawyer watched him stalking down the street, his arms waving, his tall, dark figure like some avenging angel of the night.

16

Several days passed without incident. The town was quiet and as the weather got hotter and drier, the place seemed more lethargic than ever. Dogs lay in the shade of the buildings and the wind blew up little spirals of dust that settled everywhere and left the mouth dry and sour. There was not a cloud in the sky, just a brazen orb that cast harsh shadows across Benson's Butte.

The marshal appeared to be taking things easily. He noted the glum face of the banker and greeted him when they met with a certain inner amusement. Ma Riley was also unhappy, mourning the loss of days that might have been. Her saloon was no longer a welcome place for Mr Hackman.

The marshal enquired each day after the health of Bill Quince. The man was hobbling round his sickroom on crutches now and was eating well. He would soon be ready to travel.

No more had been heard of the sheriff although Sam Benson was rumoured to have been seen riding towards Cheyenne. Matt Sawyer watched events with a detached air. He had made all his plans and only had to wait.

It was Sunday when things reached a head. The morning was bright and sharp; the butte stood black against the horizon, and the regular churchgoers were blasting out a ragged chorus of one of Moody and Sankey's new hymns.

A flash of light suddenly etched itself on the wall of the jailhouse, clear through the window like a tiny sunbeam. The marshal looked out and, at the far end of the street, he could see the tall figure of Macy leaning over a fence and flashing a mirror that picked up the rays of the sun and sent a clear signal across town. Matt Sawyer gave a grunt of satisfaction and strapped on his Colt. He reached out for the shotgun, but changed his mind. He put on his hat and made sure that his badge was clearly in view on his waistcoat. The time had come to settle matters.

He walked slowly down the main street and people on the sidewalk watched his movements with a certain fascination. Matt was not returning their greetings, not noticing his friends, but walking slowly and purposefully towards Macy's corral.

When he got there, a horse was already saddled and a pair of saddle-bags was laid across its back. A roll of blankets was tied behind the cantle and Macy leaned against the fence, a neutral but interested spectator.

'Where is he?' the marshal asked tautly.

'In the barn,' the smith answered. 'He's got a gun, Matt.'

'I know that.'

The marshal stood about fifteen feet away from the tethered horse and patiently waited the arrival of the owner. He came limping out of the barn, a slim figure in a tartan shirt and leather waistcoat.

It was Bill Quince. He carried a gun on his right hip and wore large spurs that rattled at each step.

'Mornin', Bill,' Matt Sawyer said politely.

The man halted in his tracks, still twenty feet away from the horse. He was surprised to see the lawman there.

'Mornin', Marshal,' he answered. 'Didn't expect to see you around so early in the mornin'.'

'Oh, the hymn-singin' got me outa bed. Goin' some place?'

The younger man grinned. 'Well, my leg's better so I reckon I'd best be on my way.'

'The county sheriff has a warrant out for you.'

'Sure, I know that, but I didn't think you'd be too fussed if I wasn't around to wait for him. All the news is that he's got other worries. I don't matter much any more.'

Matt Sawyer moved a step nearer. 'That's probably true. The county sheriff picked himself a heap of trouble by goin' out to Sam Benson's place and shootin' it up. He's kinda hot-headed.'

'I hear the Bensons ran him outa town.'

'Somethin' like that but it doesn't mean you can leave.'

Bill Quince moved a little nearer to his horse, and both men noticed that a collection of townspeople were gathering at a safe distance. There was a sort of tension in the air that everybody recognized.

'I don't see what's stoppin' me leavin',' Quince said edgily.

'I am.'

'You haven't got your shotgun, Marshal.'

'I don't need it, son. Just unfasten that belt and then walk quietly to the jailhouse. That way, you and me won't fall out.'

'And if I don't?'

'Then I'll kill you.'

Bill Quince was silent for a moment. 'I like you, Marshal,' he said quietly, 'and I've no quarrel with you or anybody in this town. I'm not a boastin' man but I reckon I can out-draw anybody in Benson's Butte. I don't want to kill you, so just let me pass and I'll be out of your hair and the county sheriff can do the huntin'.'

'This ain't the county sheriff's affair Bill; it's my front porch you're foulin'. I'm arrestin' you for the murder of the man who called himself Cyrus B. Sedgewick. You'll be tried in Cheyenne most likely, but it's my job to take you in.'

The crowd was gathering closer now and Macy was standing with his mouth wide open. One of his kids ran into the house to tell the rest of the family what was happening.

'Marshal,' Bill Quince said with sweet reason, 'Sedgewick was bushwhacked along with me. I was shot . . . you seen the wound . . . '

'Sure I did son. You were shot with a

.41 calibre bullet. That don't come from any pistol a cowpoke would use. It came from a derringer such as Sedgewick carried under his fancy coat.'

Quince's eyes narrowed. 'How do you figure that?' he asked.

'Because Sedgewick had a few spare bullets in his pocket. They were .41 calibre. There were also slight smears of gun oil on the linin' of his coat. We're not hicks just because we live in a small town. We got reasonin' powers, same as the city folk. There never was a bushwhackin'. I'd guess that you and your partner had a fallin' out and somebody pulled a gun. Your horse was close up to the gig when he fired and his derringer left powder burns on your pants. You fired from the saddle and hit him in the chest. You killed him, boy, as sure as the sun will shine tomorrow.'

Quince opened his mouth to say something and then changed his mind. He glanced at the distance he was from the horse and then back at the marshal.

'Drop the belt,' Matt Sawyer said sharply.

'He drew first.'

The marshal smiled. The man had confessed in front of the whole town.

'You can tell that to the judge.'

'And what good will that do? The county sheriff has a warrant out for me. Two charges of murder will be more than enough to make it a hangin' case. There's only one way out for me, Marshal. I'm gettin' on that horse and leavin' town.'

'I don't reckon so. You only have two ways of leavin' Benson's Butte, son. One is in a pine box and the other is under guard to Cheyenne courthouse.'

'It was a fair fight. He drew first.' The man's voiced was desperate.

'What was the row about? The money you got from Hackman?'

'He was cheatin' me. He always cheated me.'

'So you killed him, stole his watch and money . . . '

'No. I took the watch and chain and

the money in his wallet, but that was all he had. I reckoned he owed me. The money he got in town wasn't there. He cheated me right to the end. It's hid away someplace.'

The marshal nodded his satisfaction. 'And after you'd killed him, you found yourself in one hell of a mess. He'd shot you bad in the leg and you needed a doctor real urgent. So you had to come back to town and tell us that you'd been held up. I found the watch in your saddle-bag the other day. And the money from his wallet. Then I rode out to where you said it all happened. There were no fresh traces of a gig or a bunch of horses. No blood or tracks behind the rocks. Nothin'. You're a bad liar, boy. I had you marked down as guilty the moment I saw those bullets in his pocket. So just drop the belt and let's go get some breakfast.'

'I don't want to kill an old man . . . ' Quince's voice was rasping. He moved nearer his horse and his right hand went down towards the holster. The marshal's hand moved and the cow-poke's reaction was instant. He drew the heavy Colt and cocked it at lightning speed.

A single shot rang out. Birds scattered from the rooftops as several horses whinnied their fright.

Bill Quince moved forward a step or so. There was a slight flow of blood from the centre of his chest and as he pitched forward on his face the gaping hole in his back made it clear that the wound was fatal. The marshal's gun was wreathed in a thinning plume of smoke.

'Go get the doctor,' Matt Sawyer ordered Macy.

The man scampered off clumsily along the street and met the medical man before he had gone many paces. Doc Merton bent over the body and then stood up, dusting his pants.

'Good shooting, Matt,' he said quietly. 'Dead as mutton, if you'll pardon such an expression in cow country.'

'I didn't want to kill him,' the marshal said sadly.

'You can't reason with some people. They think they can shoot their way out of anything. So take a drink, Matt. This is a job for the mortician.'

The marshal scooped up the dead man's gun and slowly walked away from the scene. The townspeople nodded their heads or smiled encouragingly as he passed them. One or two of the men raised their hats as a sign of respect.

'Good shootin',' somebody said in a loud voice, and the words were repeated all along the street. Matt Sawyer entered his office and sat down heavily. He had never liked killing people, even when they were the lowest rogues in the territory. He unslung his belt and hung it on the usual hook. Quince's Colt lay on the desk and he picked it up and opened the gate cover to eject the cartridges one by one. The man had been a safety-conscious gun-handler and there were five bullets in the six chambers. They tumbled around the desk top and one rolled on to the floor.

The marshal pulled back the hammer to examine it with a wry smile on his face. There was no firing pin left. When Bill Quince was taken to the doctor's house with his leg wound, Matt Sawyer had moved the man's horse and equipment to Macy's smithy for storage. Being a cautious man, he had taken a large file and rasped away the firing pin. Not very sporting, but a lot safer than trying to beat a professional gun-handler to the draw.

He put the coffee pot on the stove and sat back in his chair with a feeling of quiet content. The theodolite box lay in front of him and he pulled it gently nearer. Nobody else had noticed that the instrument was a little small for such a big case. The marshal removed the theodolite for the umpteenth time and pulled at the blue velvet lining at the rear of the box. It came away in his hand and left an extra inch and a half of space.

It was Cyrus B Sedgewick's private bank. The bundles of ten-dollar bills were there, just as they had been handed over by Mr Hackman. There was also a roll of five-dollar pieces and another $3,000 in larger banknotes.

Marshal Sawyer was going to have a happy retirement.

THE END

We do hope that you have enjoyed reading this large print book.

Did you know that all of our titles are available for purchase?

We publish a wide range of high quality large print books including:
Romances, Mysteries, Classics
General Fiction
Non Fiction and Westerns

Special interest titles available in large print are:
The Little Oxford Dictionary
Music Book, Song Book
Hymn Book, Service Book

Also available from us courtesy of Oxford University Press:
Young Readers' Dictionary
(large print edition)
Young Readers' Thesaurus
(large print edition)

For further information or a free brochure, please contact us at:
Ulverscroft Large Print Books Ltd.,
The Green, Bradgate Road, Anstey,
Leicester, LE7 7FU, England.
Tel: (00 44) **0116 236 4325**
Fax: (00 44) **0116 234 0205**